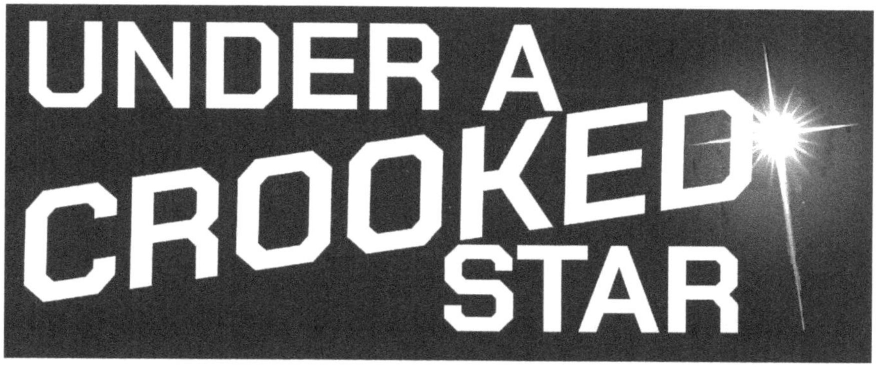

Airship 27 Productions

Under a Crooked Star

Published by Airship 27 Productions
www.airship27.com
www.airship27hangar.com

Editor: Ron Fortier
Associate Editor: Jonathan Sweet
Marketing and Promotions Manager: Michael Vance
Production Designer: Rob Davis

ISBN: 978-1-969285-11-0

Produced in the United States of America

10 9 8 7 6 5 4 3 2 1

UNDER A *CROOKED* STAR

by Daniel Whiston

CHAPTER 1: DOWN IN THE HEIGHTS

Earth, Sol System, 2351

The trouble with suckers is there's never enough of them.

Neroy Sphinx shuffled the Centauri cards and sighed. The mark had wandered into the bar alone. A group would have let Neroy work the table safely. Instead, he was having to do it one-to-one. Risky. But despite his best efforts, the guy still hadn't noticed Neroy was cheating.

He was going to have to make it more obvious.

Neroy carried on shuffling, drawing it out.

"Hurry up and deal before I die of old age," complained the mark.

Neroy dealt the pack. "Dying old shouldn't be a worry for you, pal. Not with a sweet tone like that."

The man grunted and grabbed his cards. A stranger with serious creds was unusual in Neroy's favourite bar; the area was such a backwater. Even Neroy wasn't too sure exactly where the place was, sometimes. When he was having a bad day. But not today. Today was a good day.

Slowly and obviously, Neroy reached out and palmed a winCrystal. Nothing happened. Neroy thought he was going to have to do it again, then the bulky guy's brain caught up with his eyes.

He leapt up. "You're a cheating sonofabitch! I saw that!"

Neroy shrugged. "Sorry, pal, thought it was mine from the last hand. My mistake. Apologies—the pot's yours." Good, the guy was sitting back down, sipping his drink again. And now he'd put his glass down near the edge of the table. Perfect.

"Here you go," said Neroy, shoving the pile of cred-Wafers just clumsily enough to knock the guy's synthiAle into his lap. His face went red and he started sputtering, but Neroy calmed him down and got him a fresh drink. Then he offered to take the damp seat himself. They shuffled round the table until the guy was sitting with his back to the bar's sole functioning holoScreen. It was lucky even that one was working, Neroy thought. The joint was one of the cruddiest dives in Terminus City, which had to make it one of the cruddiest bars on Earth.

Still, he had the mark where he needed him now.

The trouble was that the guy hadn't wanted to sit with his back to the door. So he'd been facing the holoScreen, showing his hand to the rear wall. Instead of to the lensPixels Neroy had activated in the holoScreen, after the barman had told him there was a high roller in the place. An old trick, but the software was easy enough to hack on obsolete models. Neroy had picked up the technique somewhere, but he couldn't quite remember where.

Not that it mattered, because the mark's hand was splashing up on Neroy's dataLens now that the guy was sitting in front of the Screen. The feed was patchy, but the icons and card colours were coming through just fine. Centauri was a complex game. Too complicated for regular cheating. But seeing the other guy's cards would do the trick.

Neroy went in high and folded when he didn't have to, before going all-in on the next round. He could see the mark's mind working it over, trying to gauge just how scatty Neroy really was. Neroy drained his glass and made himself go a little cross-eyed, belched loudly and scratched his ass. The mark whacked down a fresh stack of creds and sneered. Neroy smiled back. The guy was just the kind of sucker he liked. Overconfident, unobservant and right in front of him.

Two minutes later, Neroy had all the money on the table.

He tensed a little as he raked in the creds. The mark looked desperate, like they always did when they'd lost money they couldn't afford to. Probably wasn't even his.

"Listen-" he spat, but Neroy didn't let him get any further.

"Who wants a drink?" yelled Neroy. A group of regulars crowded round, and the joint's hulking barman rolled over with a tray of glasses. Neroy took one and raised it, to toast his benefactor.

But the man had gone.

Outside the bar Neroy leant on the composite wall and took a drag on his smoke. He exhaled slowly, watching a ship pass overhead in the night sky. It was titanic, an industrial-metallic shard that looked like a factory wrapped around a skyscraper, ponderously clawing up and away from Katari Spaceport.

Times were hard, and the Peach Heights district was too impoverished to be able to afford a quietFly field. Even at this distance, the thundering engines shook the sky. The ship was moving slowly, but it would be out over the ocean soon. Terminus City was ten times bigger than Old New York had ever been, from the western radDeserts to the Dead Atlantic, but once the ship was high enough to turn on its ion drive it would vanish in seconds. Neroy didn't know when he'd last felt like this. Gambling for real money, conning someone who deserved it. It meant a lot. Right now, it felt like it meant everything.

The ship had gone, leaving the sky to the distant outline of the Candrassian

Order's Mother Temple. Lacking external illumination, the mountainous structure dominated the nocturnal skyline in a negative sense, occluding the lights of the megaBlocks that lay behind it in the cityCore. A missing tooth in the city's night-time grimace.

Neroy began to feel uneasy. The card game's rush was fading, satisfaction twisting into an unfamiliar hunger to push things further. Why had he left the mark with any money at all? The thought of finding the guy and picking his pocket came out of nowhere. With a stab of panic he pushed it away. Where had that come from? What kind of person would want to risk doing something like that?

Neroy pushed off from the wall. He felt better once he was back inside. The bar was a little beat up, like a lot of places these days. But with the gloLights down low it was nice and cosy. Neroy took a drink to a quiet corner and sank into a patched-up gelCouch. He closed his eyes, looking forward to thinking about nothing at all. Neroy heard footsteps approach, but didn't crack an eyelid. He knew the barman well enough to tell him he didn't need anything else, without standing on ceremony.

A rough kick smacked the side of his foot.

It was the mark. Looking up at the guy made him seem bigger, and he'd been sturdy enough to begin with. Even in the dim light, Neroy could see his face was flushed.

"Hey, pal," Neroy said. "Pull up a seat. Relax. You look red as a beet, and about as appetising."

"Shut up!" The guy gripped an empty bottle by the neck. "I need my damn money back. Now!"

Neroy's mouth was dry. He searched for something to say, but a dizzy nausea scrambled his thoughts. He felt odd again, like he had outside. A sensation he would have described, had anyone asked, as feeling the presence of a part of himself that wasn't there.

The mark smashed the end of the bottle against the table. Neroy threw his arms in front of his face.

"Give me my money back!" screamed the mark.

The man jabbed at Neroy with his makeshift weapon. Neroy cringed as he closed in, but behind the mark something was moving, almost too fast to see.

It was the barman, running in a blur which terminated in a crunching impact that knocked the guy flat. Before Neroy had time to get up, the barman was dragging the mark out of the place. Then he returned, clucking over Neroy like a mother hen. Neroy let him fuss. The guy was a regular guardian angel, always looking out for him. Heart of gold, and for a follower of the Candrassian Order he was actually a great drinking buddy. Neroy had known him for years now.

Then things darkened as the strange feelings kicked off again. Neroy was seized by the odd notion that this sort of thing happened to him all the time. But that wasn't right, he knew it wasn't.

A beautiful woman at the bar was striving to make herself unobtrusively noticeable. Neroy seized on the distraction. A delicate rose tattoo curved around her face, clashing slightly with her yellow cat's-eyes implants. She was a working girl the barman tolerated, and they talked from time to time. In fact, now Neroy considered it, he'd actually known her for a few years.

"Get you a drink, honey?" Neroy asked, signalling the barman.

"Isn't that supposed to be my line?" she replied. "*Buy a girl a beer, baby?* That kind of thing?"

Neroy fished out his smokes. She took one without asking. He lit them both and they chatted, mostly street talk. Her world was comfortingly familiar. After a while Neroy got them another round. The joint was quieter now, and she wasn't likely to pick up any more trade. Neroy took out the mark's credWafers and slid them along the bar.

"Here. I've taken up a lot of your time tonight. Why don't you go home a little early." Truth was, he didn't want the money any more.

She smiled, and took the creds. "Thanks, Neroy. But that kind of money buys you a lot more time with me. Much as you want. Hell, for a skinny guy in a crumpled suit, you're kind of cute. Some girls even like a man with a touch of white at the temples. Lends a little gravitas."

"Heh. It's the price of wisdom, honey."

She brushed the back of his hand with her fingertips. "Why not come back to my place? It isn't far."

Neroy smiled, shaking his head. "No need. Hell, it wasn't my money for very long. Some might say it wasn't really mine at all."

The girl pouted. "It's not every day you've got money to spend on me, Neroy. Maybe I want you to remember me the next time."

Neroy shook his head again, but without so much of the smile. "I don't have it in me these days."

She dropped the pout and held his gaze. "I'm not talking about having it in you. I'm talking about you putting it in me. How long's it been, Neroy? Years?"

She kept her hand on his and he felt desire stir, for the first time he could remember, mixed up with the adrenalin and the con and everything else. But it was a fragile thing, quick to gutter and die. The girl carried on talking softly, but he wasn't listening. Something about the bar was coming into focus.

He realised he'd been feeling it for a little while tonight, in different ways. It wasn't just one thing. It was the staging of the scene. The con game. The improvised swapping of seats, saying one thing while planning another. The sudden flash of violence. It all felt deeply familiar, somehow. Too familiar. And the woman's attention. That felt familiar too, everything reminding him of something he just couldn't place.

The bar's front door crashed open with a loud bang.

The mark staggered back in looking unhinged, face badly swollen from his previous ejection. In his hand he held a blaster. He raised a shaking hand to point it at Neroy.

"Give me my money back, you bastard!"

Neroy felt something hurtle by. He thought the mark had shot at him, but then he saw the barman, halfway to the door. Moving impossibly fast. But not quite fast enough.

The mark just managed to bring his gun to bear before the barman slammed into him. They struggled, then a pulse of blinding light punched through the bar's window. The blaster must have been on a kinetic setting, because it didn't melt a neat little hole. The massive pane shattered, fragments exploding out into the street.

The barman gripped the now unconscious assailant's gun and squeezed. There was a crunching noise as pieces of its casing snapped off and fell to the floor. Neroy just had time to wonder why no one had ever told him the barman had military-grade enhancements, before a huge shard of glass fell from the window frame. It hit the ground, exploding into a spray of tiny slivers that shot out across the bar. Pain nicked his cheek.

And with that, he remembered.

Pushed too far by one final shock, the memory block cracked. The familiar feeling of the con, the woman's touch and all the rest of it had pushed him right up against the barrier, and now it fractured. He remembered. Remembered that he used to be someone else, someone more than this pale version of himself. Someone stronger. Cleverer, more guileful. Someone in control. Not someone trapped within himself, inexplicably less than he should have been.

But in that instant of clarity, he also somehow knew, with a surge of horror, that the realisation would be fleeting. Already it was starting to fade, like a dream you just couldn't hold on to.

Through the shattered window, pinpricks of light were visible far, far up against the distant blackness. They used to be his, Neroy thought. He used to live amongst the stars, and someone had taken it all away from him. But no. Not just that. Something had happened to him out there. Something awful. For a split second he was seized by utter terror, formless and inescapable.

Then the horror was gone.

For the brief moment he had left, still truly himself, Neroy looked up at the stars. Tears wetted his cheeks. But then all he could see was the darkness between them, a darkness that reached down and touched him, flowing inside him and covering everything up again, until he had no idea what he was doing just standing there, looking up into the cold night sky like some idiot.

"Hey, Neroy," came a soft voice.

It was the barman. Neroy wiped his face. "Must have gotten something in my eye."

There was a drink for him on the bar. Next to it, a narcPack.

"Got something special for you, Neroy. Take the edge right off. Just how you like it."

Neroy slumped on a stool and accepted a light from the barman. He chased the narcPack with the drink, and when the glass was empty the barman conjured up another.

"Gonna have to review security," the barman muttered. "This place is supposed to be real quiet. A refuge. If anything happened to you tonight, I'd have been in serious trouble with my supervisor. As it is, I'd better give him a quick update. Mr G likes to stay in the loop. But anyway, I think you've had more than enough excitement. Stuff like this just doesn't happen here. And believe you me, it isn't gonna happen again."

A mild frown crossed Neroy's face. How the barman had put that had sounded a little odd. But then the warm feeling from the drink and the narc made the contents of the holoScreen much more interesting.

Tinkling ice announced the arrival of another drink.

"Everything OK, Neroy?" asked the barman. "You looked a little troubled before. Something wrong?"

Neroy absently picked up his glass, eyes fixed on the gently glowing Screen.

"I don't remember."

CHAPTER 2: INTERSTITIAL

Candrassian Order Mother Temple, Earth, 2357

Clarence Griffin sighed at the sound of footsteps drawing near. He turned away from the panoramic view of Terminus City, spread out below his vantage point at the apex of the Candrassian Order's Mother Temple. An Acolyte was approaching across the white vastness of the Temple's pinnacle level. Fajid, one of the newer initiates.

Griffin sighed again. Why must he endure these constant interruptions? Grumpily, he pointed his old man's cane towards the nearest Cloister Nest. The Nests, conversation pits sunk into the pinnacle level's floor, provided private spaces for reflection and discussion. Griffin began to walk across the promenade.

Then halted.

Fajid had frozen at the Cloister Nest steps, by one of the armoured plaSteel display cases scattered throughout the Temple. Griffin tensed. Fajid stood stiff and silent. The artefacts constrained within the cases shared a blackened, broken appearance, as though scorched on the site of some ancient battlefield. But they had been inert for years now. Fajid shuddered, then was still again.

A torrent of blood erupted from her mouth.

Instantly, a haze of small black particles manifested around Griffin's hands. The swarm of miniature sunspots oscillated around his fingertips, ready to channel his abilities in a variety of lethal ways, should circumstances demand it.

Fajid collapsed to her knees, choking. Dark fluid spattered the ivory floor as she vomited. Blood began streaming from her eyes as her fingers scrabbled at her jaw. She pitched over. Fajid's back arched against the ground, compressing her into an agonisingly contorted pose, shaking as though electrocuted.

Then she collapsed; a broken mess.

Griffin stared at the pool of blood as people rushed to help, then carried Fajid's dripping body away, the black particles fading from his hands as the danger passed. A slight motion caught his eye. The red fluid was flowing slowly down the slight curvature of the floor towards the Cloister Nest. It ran down the Nest's stairs in rivulets that crossed over each other to form a complex, organic pattern.

At first it seemed chaotic. Then, in a sudden, arresting Insight, he grasped its meaning, beyond doubt. Terror possessed him for the first time in ten years. He closed his eyes and deepened his breathing. Gradually his heart slowed, and-

Griffin jumped as something touched him.

It was Brother Azrael, a Senior Administrator. "Are you all right, Mr Griffin?"

"Yes, indeed, brother," responded Griffin. "Merely shaken."

Azrael's eyes were brimming. "Poor Fajid. Such a precious young lady."

"Oh, indeed," Griffin said. "A tragic loss." He frowned. "She made the most wonderful tea."

Brother Azrael stared at Griffin, but held his reply.

Griffin and Azrael descended into the Nest, careful to avoid the blood. They sank into a gelCouch. Griffin contemplated the crimson mess as he stroked his goatee beard. Mirrorlike, the blood reflected his ebony fingers resting amongst the white tufts on his chin. On the surface, it appeared merely a glistening spray of blood. An abstract biological pattern. But his Vision had taken him beneath, to the true meaning it contained.

Hidden subtleties within the oozing streams revealed the form of a familiar Star System, and within it, a hidden maw, sealed these past ten years but now agape once more. The Great Arterial Link to the other side of the galaxy had re-opened.

Damnation awaited them all.

"Thank you for giving me a moment, Brother," Griffin said. "It was much needed, for I fear I have seen a Portent. A Sign, written in blood."

"A sign?" Azrael whispered, wide-eyed.

"Indeed," replied Griffin. "Drimimancy. Divination through blood." He reflected on the Portent's meaning. Mankind had only once visited the vastly distant planet he thought of as The Cursed Orb. It lurked far beyond the human worlds at the other end of the Arterial Link, a wormhole leading to the galaxy's far side. The Link was intermittently accessible from human space via the Kumeiijm'a System, but had last opened a decade ago. The Orb was a trap, set by mocking Ancients who saw humanity as vassals at best—prey at worst. A trap he had escaped only through terrible sacrifice.

The memory of what he had been forced to do out there made him shudder. He pushed it away. He and the other survivors had fled back to human space, sealing the Great Link behind them, leaving the Ancients and the Dark Shapes that flitted around them far behind. But now the Link was apparently open once more. And Hell awaited.

"What, exactly, has been revealed?" Azrael asked.

Griffin seized his cane. "The end of humanity has re-awoken! A threat that has slept these past ten years. An eternity of burning torment for every man, woman, and child. Damnation!"

Azrael blanched. "Surely not, Mr Griffin? I appreciate yours is the boon of Prophecy, but might there not be some other interpretation, a nuance perhaps, that-"

"No! There is no mistake." Griffin stabbed his stick towards the display case where Fajid had collapsed. It contained a small, skeletal object, spindly legs spreading out from a central cluster, its techno-organic curvature profoundly unnatural, and painful to look at.

"That artefact was retrieved from Kumeiijm'a," he continued, "whose System contains the gateway to an impossibly distant Star System. I saw the Kumeiijm'a System—just now—in my Vision. It is no coincidence that the Acolyte's seizure was triggered by proximity to the artefact. The exotic particle stream that must now be flowing once more through the Great Link has somehow reached us, in a manner we do not understand. And yet which has given us a Sign."

"But still, Mr Griffin', countered Azrael. "An eternity of torment?" He looked suddenly hopeful. "You are speaking spiritually, perhaps?"

"No," sighed Griffin. "Sadly not..." A Gifting from himself to Azrael would provide the man with a full appreciation of the situation. It would also require a significant expenditure of psychic energy on Griffin's part. But it was necessary. There was much that must now be done, and he required support from Activist factions within the Order, such as Azrael's.

Griffin took the other man's hand. The terrible memories flowed from his mind to Azrael's, and *<<the pain from the flames was unbelievable make it stop stop stop please, a world on fire, Hellfire, scalding hot, his friends screaming, thrashing, evil laughter everywhere, mocking their pain, taking delight in it, cherishing it, make it stop stop stop please just>>*

Gently, Griffin withdrew. Azrael was hyperventilating, eyes unfocused.

"These last ten years we have waited here on a diminished Earth, humanity's brotherhood reduced from its heights through man's own folly," Griffin intoned. "Earth's remit no longer runs beyond the Solar System. Man bickers with himself. There is no one to help us... so we must help ourselves."

Azrael's jaw trembled. "But how?" He pointed at the artefact. "Is that... thing the key to this?"

Griffin shook his head. "No. Rather, there is a man. A man whose destiny was entwined with the threat we face, from the very beginning. Signs and Portents have revealed he must be part of any solution."

For a moment, Griffin regretted burdening Azrael with the Gifting. The man was terrified. But no. He needed support, for what lay ahead. Which required sharing at least part of the truth more widely within the Order. Time was short.

"Who is this man?" Azrael asked, voice quavering.

Griffin frowned. "For the past ten years he has languished, a shadow of himself, the spark within him kept dim for fear of consuming him, through unbearable guilt for what has gone before."

"He was involved in this damnation threat... from the beginning?"

"Indeed," Griffin replied. "However, he does not know the role he must play, nor even who he truly is... but now the slumberer must awaken."

"Is he of the Order?"

Griffin coughed. "Ah, no. He is... of a more temporal nature. Years ago, I knew him well. To play his role, he must regain what was taken from him in order to save his sanity. Otherwise, his mind would have been destroyed by the horrors he witnessed. But now he must regain his memories. And become whole." Griffin steepled his fingers. "We face a puzzle of fiendish complexity.

We shall need his Insights. His intuition. But his recovery cannot be rushed..."

Griffin gave Azrael his instructions. There was a doctor to contact, to initiate the necessary procedures, in coordination with a barman from the Peach Heights district. Griffin hadn't communicated with the bartender directly since a security report six years previously, involving an angry Centauri player with a blaster. But that should mean all had subsequently been well.

"Medical science will start this journey," Griffin cautioned. "But only the power of the Order can complete it, without distorting his essential nature, so that his true persona may re-emerge." Griffin stared past Azrael, seeing a man who wasn't there.

"We can only pray his soul remains pure."

CHAPTER 3: ONE LAST JOB

Terminus City, Earth

Neroy Sphinx let the weight of the gun drag his hand down towards the hotel room floor. He slumped back in the chair he'd jerked awake in a couple of seconds ago. The weapon's explosive discharge was an awful ringing in his ears, and there was a sharp ache in his wrist.

The blast had bitten a chunk out of the doorframe behind the man he'd just shot at. A trickle of blood from the thug's ear had reached the guy's collar. Only a nick, but it was bleeding bad. A sudden wave of panic overwhelmed him. Where the hell was he?

"Maybe you didn't hear me the first time," the injured man drawled.

An even bigger guy who had to be Bloody Ear's partner lumbered past him into the room. They both drew enormous hand cannons that only someone with an augmented musculature would be able to use, and pointed them at him in an artificially synchronised motion.

"Our employer would like a word with you," said Bloody Ear. "If you don't mind."

The door looked flimsy enough for the guy to have walked right through it. Man like him would have all the prime physical and tactical enhancements. But instead he'd messed around with the lock, giving Neroy time to jolt awake, fumble for the weapon he'd picked up from some guy in a club last night and get off a surprisingly accurate shot. Given the room was still spinning a little. The club last night. He remembered something else he'd picked up there.

Neroy dropped the gun and scrabbled for the bottle under his chair. Empty, damn it. He patted himself down for smokes, locating them in his back pocket. There was nothing about guys like this he could use. But the man who'd sent them? He wanted something. And that would present an angle in due course.

"Love to oblige you boys, truly I would," Neroy began. Buy some time, find a gap somewhere, squeeze through it. "The person who wants to see me, obviously wants to see me in person. But shouldn't you be asking for ID or something? I mean, I could be anyone..."

Bloody Ear's pal bulldozed over to Neroy. He hoisted him up, granite fists grating against Neroy's chest.

"OK. Are you Neroy Sphinx?" Bigger Guy asked. "He was the man we were told to bring back in one piece."

Neroy smiled the widest grin he could muster. "The one and only."

The heavy dropped Neroy back in his seat, knocking the wind out of him. Suddenly feeling terminally short of breath, the walls came crashing in. *"Are you Neroy Sphinx?"* Yes. Yes, he was. But who the hell was that? There'd been a hospital. Last night. He'd been ill. But it was a feverish blur. A bad dream. Push back further. Drinking, gambling. A quiet little neighbourhood in Peach Heights, the rundown district next to the hospital. A bar. A cruddy apartment. He knew it well. Too damn well. He'd been living there for years. But it somehow felt like an existence he'd only been half awake for. For a long time.

Then he jolted. Like he'd walked into a wall of dark glass. Because before Peach Heights there was... a big chunk of nothing. Years wide, years deep. He could almost see the gap in his memories, a dark presence defined by its absence. But when he tried to focus on it his awareness slid off, reflecting back at him, like he was looking into a dark mirror that a chunk of his memories were hidden behind.

Whatever the barrier was, it squatted between his recent faded half-life and what had come before. Because on the other side of the inaccessible part of his memories concealed behind the Cold Black Glass was another, earlier life. Not fuzzy. Faint, but real. Sharpening by the second as he-

Bloody Ear snapped his fingers in Neroy's face. "Keep it together, Sphinx. Don't spin out."

"Heavy night?" asked Bigger Guy, laying down a large equipment case Neroy hadn't noticed before.

Yes. Yes, it had been. He suddenly recalled that he'd needed one.

"I... had an awful nightmare last night," Neroy replied. Momentarily, a sense of utter terror *twisted* inside him. Then it vanished, almost before he'd registered it. Neroy swallowed hard. "Don't remember the details. Just woke up in hospital, totally afraid."

Bigger Guy snickered, but screw him. Neroy needed to follow the thread.

"I... slipped out, and hit a club. Hard. Then... I'm not sure. Guess I ended up here. How the hell did you guys find me? Even I didn't know where I was..."

Bloody Ear's reply sent a jolt down Neroy's spine. "Boss Dubblz has the best snifferRoutines money can buy, Sphinx."

Dubblz. He knew that name.

"Always on the lookout for personnel, is Boss D," Bloody Ear continued. "So when you booked into this dive under your own name? Data feed lit up like a regular little solar flare." He lifted something dangerous-looking out of the equipment case. "You've been out of circulation a long time, Sphinx. But not long enough we're gonna forget about prime talent like you."

Bigger Guy leant over until his face was uncomfortably close. His breath was stale, lifeless. Neroy forced himself not to turn away. "Mr Dubblz is planning on retiring," Bigger Guy said. "But there's one last job he wants to pull first. You remember Mr Dubblz, don't you?"

Neroy made himself grin. "Sure I remember him. Little fuzzy on details, but I'm sure they'll come back." But the details weren't fuzzy at all. The name Dubblz was familiar from back before his ghostly Peach Heights life, and the Cold Black Glass that abutted it. Minor gangster who probably wasn't so minor anymore, since that was... how long ago?

Neroy accessed earthNet to check the dates. There was a lag as his dataLink implant meshed with the local nodeStream. Ancient piece of crap. Diagnostics said it hadn't been upgraded for years. The flow stabilised, and the visuals updated in Neroy's dataLens. Then the room spun, and kept on spinning until the nails he'd dug into the palm of his hand drew blood.

Fifteen years.

He'd last met Dubblz fifteen years ago. 2342. Just a small-time hood he'd done a job with. But the year he'd last seen Dubblz was followed by a blank half-decade—the Cold Black Glass. Then ten blurry years in Peach Heights that, according to his online Hab records, began in 2347. Ten years that felt like a dream. Warm and cosy, like cheap opiates.

The sound of a weapon being cocked brought him back to the hotel room.

The thing from the case was a cross between a rifle and a surgical tool with a gun-like hand grip and a long, tapering snout terminating in a needle so sharp his eyes slid right off the end of it.

"Now listen," Neroy floundered, "I'm sure Boss Dubblz didn't go to all the trouble-"

"Bend over," Bloody Ear growled. Neroy knew there was nothing to be gained by arguing. He had nowhere to go.

Neroy got up and turned around, resting his hands on the chair. "Listen, let's just-"

A shock of pain took Neroy's breath away as an industrial-sized needle stabbed his backside. Through the agony, he felt something solid injected into him, a tiny fragment of something hard. Then the needle was roughly yanked out. He yelped, but when the pain retreated, he couldn't feel the fragment any more.

"What did you do to me?" Neroy wailed.

"Nothing to worry about, Sphinx," Bloody Ear chuckled. "Long as you don't screw up. Just a little guarantee. You know, for good behaviour."

Neroy felt icy cold. "What did you put in me?" He didn't want to, but he couldn't stop himself from clamping his hands over his throbbing buttock.

"Small microbomb, inert until primed by a trigger code." Bloody Ear shrugged with a mighty roll of his shoulders. "Still, could have been worse."

"How? How exactly could it be worse?"

"With the last guy, Boss D put it in himself. But he didn't ask the guy to turn around first. I tell ya, I almost threw up."

Neroy jumped down from the thugs' shuttle, which had come to land under a looming expressway. The windows were opaqued, so he had no idea where they'd flown to. Wherever it was it was cold, air heavy with the threat of rain.

"Over there," said Bigger Guy, shoving Neroy towards a huddle of abandoned buildings by a dilapidated factory.

Despite everything, Neroy smiled. He was waking up, everything coming into focus. How he felt now was close to his recollections of fifteen years ago. Before the Cold Black Glass, and the fuzzy years after the Glass in Peach Heights that stretched out, vague and hazy, from the near side of the gaping hole in his memories until just a few hours ago.

A street stall was coming up, a half dome with an open front, selling drinks and narcPacks. A hacked-together thermal regulator at the back kept everything at the right temperature, its leaky rubber piping draped over obsolete display cabinets plastered with faded, ancient posters for drinks and snack products.

The stall was run by a scrawny girl with a shaved head and crude, angular facial tattoos. She smiled at Neroy.

"Got any Galacti Joos cartons, honey?" asked Neroy, pointing at a dusty poster. His mouth was sandpaper-dry. She shook her head, no. Of course not. Altarian joosBerries cost a fortune these days. It occurred to Neroy that almost all the adverts were for dead product lines, things that had relied on cheap imports during the EarthFed era. Things that simply weren't available now, hadn't been for ten years, ever since—what did they call it—*The Fall of '47.*

That was it. The Fall of EarthFed, when the Earth-centred system of trade, military cooperation, interstellar communication and everything else had come crashing down in a matter of days. His Peach Heights existence had begun at the same time as The Fall, and the resulting mega recession that Earth was still trapped in. He'd been vaguely aware of it at the time, but hadn't been interested in politics. And wherever his money had come from for the past ten years, it had never run out. So, vaguely aware was all he'd ever needed to be.

"OK, give me a Citi Ade," he smiled. "Recycled sewage water, synthetic sweeteners and borderline-legal stimulants. Everything an ageing boy needs. Actually, make it three." Neroy offered cartons to Bloody Ear and Bigger Guy, but they just glowered. He took a sip and strolled off.

He'd walked a dozen steps before he realised he was whistling.

They were nearing the abandoned buildings now, a bunch of maintenance sheds and parts stores crammed in around a larger, official-looking structure that appeared in better shape. They all had an aerospace connection. Then he saw a sign on the huge, run-down factory, still some distance away. It made shuttles.

They were somewhere in the hinterlands of the Katari Spaceport district. Past the factory, a strip of wasteland offered a glimpse of the faraway cityCore. From this distance the kilometre-high megaBlocks merged into a wall of vertical urban sprawl draped with shimmering curtains of neon from the vehicles that swarmed over them in ever-shifting constellations, as though the Northern Lights had been wrapped around a monstrous Termite's Nest.

The faded sign on the official-looking structure read *EarthFed Officer Academy*. It was shuttered, long disused. Under the sign was an inscription, carved into the lintel stone. *From Humanity's Birthplace, to the Shining Stars.* Neroy laughed. Whatever else he was, Dubblz was smart. No one was going to be using this place anytime soon.

The Academy had probably been the first place to close when everything fell apart. Terminus City had been at the centre of EarthFed for two hundred years, since someone had stumbled across the Sol System's wormhole and re-discovered Earth's lost, backwards human cousins on worlds across the quadrant. Cousins that Earth humans had never known they had, but were all too happy to sell to and dominate once they all became reacquainted.

The thought briefly stirred something inside Neroy. He'd had a life out there, before Peach Heights and the Black Glass. Neroy looked up, but all he could see were clouds.

Then it had all come crashing down in The Fall. EarthFed fell apart, just like that, and now Earth was the centre of nothing at all. Neroy looked around, but the only other thing was a tattered poster behind shattered glass: *Terminus City, Gateway to the Galaxy.*

"OK, give me a Citi Ade."

"They should call it Terminal City now," Neroy said. "Someone should put it out of its misery."

There was no response. The two men were standing perfectly still behind him, blank-faced. Bigger Guy's eyelids flickered. A rapid fluttering started in his fingers, and he raised his hand to a blank section of the wall, fingertips drumming on a section of the stone surface in an intricate, repetitive pattern. A point of pale lilac light appeared on the wall, spiking out to become a thin line that sketched the outline of a doorway onto the featureless stone.

The door slid open, revealing a dark interior.

Boss Dubblz wasn't how Neroy remembered him. He'd never been big, but something seriously wrong had happened to the wizened little old man in the throne-like hoverchair, wearing a one-piece jumpsuit that made him look like an ancient infant. The white-clad nurse in close attendance indicated that whatever had occurred had inflicted lasting medical consequences. Neroy hoped they were painful.

His recollection of Boss Dubblz's character seemed more reliable. Choked pleas. Sneering dismissal. Violent retribution. From the way Dubblz's crew were constantly on edge, the man still seemed to see people as commodities at best, vessels for terrifying punishment at worst.

Dubblz floated his chair across the spacious hall filling the bowels of the Academy, leaving his men behind. The nurse stepped forward in sync. Neroy realised she was tethered to the chair by a slender filament running into a tiny incision in her throat. Her face was a mask, eyes deadened.

"Neroy Sphinx," Dubblz smirked. "Been a long time. Glad to see you look as cruddy as always."

Neroy lit a smoke. Dubblz wanted something. The only play was to see what it was. "Yeah, well, you know how it is… one lousy day after another'll do that to a man. So how are you, Dubblz?"

"Better than you. I'd heard you were dead. You look like you've been crawling in the gutter like a crazy person."

"Kind of you to say so. Didn't think you cared. But do you mind if we cut to it? What exactly do you want?"

Dubblz leered. "You." He thumbed a control panel, and the chair descended to the floor. But it moved too suddenly for the nurse to follow the movement smoothly enough. Her throat incision started bleeding, her face remaining completely expressionless.

Dubblz levered himself hesitantly onto his feet. He stood for a moment, then paced slowly up and down, arms clasped behind his back. Neroy attempted to appear as attentive as possible.

"A priceless collection of twenty-first century art's en route to Europa City from the Antarctic Territories," Dubblz began. "It's passing through TC for forty-eight hours, in an ultraSecure private vault under a bank downtown. Priority police monitoring, designated guardDroids. You know. The works. But I want it. Problem is, cops're cracking down just now, and it's gonna be tough. Tannermann, my usual guy, he's just let me down. Badly. Divided loyalties. That's where you come in. Planners like you are hard to come by. And people always said you were the best. Born under a crooked star, crap like that. One of those savants. Super-intuitive. Well, I need you on board."

Dubblz seemed to have paused. Neroy felt it wise to take up the cue. "So what's the plan?" he asked.

Dubblz smiled a sly little grin, looking like nothing but the devil. "You tell me."

It had been fifteen minutes since Dubblz had left Neroy at his private bar and floated off to a side chamber, having told Neroy he was going to torture his predecessor Tannermann to death, following some unspecified betrayal. The torture chamber wasn't perfectly soundproofed, but Neroy had discovered through rapid experimentation that standing behind a pillar at the far end of the bar obscured the screams almost entirely. Not all of them, though, and the awful sounds were making him drink more quickly than felt wise.

The high-pitched whine of some kind of industrial saw had been particularly horrendous, preceded by desperate begging that had twisted into the most hideous screams Neroy had ever heard. Women giving birth sounded a little like that. But they didn't have people laughing at them as they shrieked.

The bar occupied a corner of a hall on a deep sub level of the Academy. The upper floors were derelict, but Boss Dubblz had converted the basement into his centre of operations. Bigger Guy and Bloody Ear had accompanied Dubblz, leaving Neroy with Dubblz's crew. Nobody seemed to mind him helping himself, so he slipped behind the bar and began fixing a fresh drink. Hadn't been any screaming for a little while, so Dubblz might return at any moment.

Neroy's hands poured and stirred as he drifted amongst the bottles. Dubblz wanted some loot, kept somewhere tricky, and he didn't know how to get it. If he did, he'd have taken it already. He'd give a lot of latitude, but under pressure, and he wouldn't have any intention of letting Neroy go, however well it went. So the bomb had to be taken care of before it all played out.

Dubblz hadn't mentioned retiring, but he clearly wasn't doing well. That meant he'd commit a decent level of resources to get what he needed. But there wasn't much time, so Dubblz wouldn't be able to check all the moving pieces. And his crew were meatheads.

"Perfect," Neroy murmured.

He inspected his glass, then sat back down next to the pillar and took a sip. Best Cosmo he'd tasted in years. Good, clean vodka, just enough lime. Exactly how he'd always liked it. He noted his long-term recall was almost perfect, now. Sharp. Detailed. All the usual memories seemed to be back, the ones that everybody had.

Parents, a homeworld. A life drifting from planet to planet. A hustler's life. Women who came and went, money that came and went too, which was fine. It always came back. Rolling from here to there, taking what he could get, becoming better at the game all the time. A solo game. Trust no one had been the first lesson. Then no one could let you down. Just roll along, watch your back and keep your eye on the main chance. Nobody else was going to do it for you.

And then, fifteen years ago, came that sudden wall of Black Glass, hiding half a decades' worth of memories until the blurry start of his Peach Heights life, ten years' back. Years that still weren't coming into focus nearly as much as his earlier life. He could remember the jobs he'd pulled way back then, and where the money had gone. Most of it on women and gambling. The rest he'd squandered. But Peach Heights was one long hungover Sunday afternoon, for ten whole years. Perhaps he'd gotten sick, a decade ago. Brain inflammation. Some kind of virus. Maybe Peach Heights was an extended convalescence from whatever illness had taken his memories.

But it felt odd he'd just accepted it for years. As though whatever had happened to him had also made him acquiesce to the memory loss. Maybe someone had intended it that way.

It had all come to an end yesterday, though. Yesterday he'd been in his regular bar, in the Heights. Someone had bought him a drink, couldn't remember who. He'd become very unwell. The hospital, later on, was a fever-blur. He'd been unconscious most of the time there, until he'd woken screaming from a hideous nightmare, the details of which he couldn't recall.

The drink in his hand was icy cold, and the chill had spread to the tips of his fingers now. Ice. There was something about ice...

He almost dropped the glass as it rose up out of nowhere.

Right before his Peach Heights memories began, right on the very edge of the Black Glass. Somewhere cold. So cold. An Ice World. And a woman. A tall woman, in black. Carefully, Neroy put the Cosmo down and closed his eyes. A headache was spiking in his temples. Gently now. There was more to come, he could feel it. But it was starting to get painful to try to -

"Too much to drink, ya feeb?" It was Dubblz. Gore spattered his fingers, and something pink glistened on one of his slippered feet. Neroy tried his best not to look at it.

"Just enough to overcome my natural bashfulness," smiled Neroy, sipping his Cosmo so he could think for a moment. Time to stop pushing at his memories. Just let it come if it wanted to. And he needed to focus exclusively on Dubblz, right now, or he wasn't going to stay alive long enough to remember anything else.

Dubblz's chair floated to the bar and someone gave him a drink. A cup, not a glass. It smelled like warm milk. "So. Tannermann let me down, but that's fine. You're a quality act, Sphinx." Dubblz beamed. "And I know you're motivated."

He tossed something tiny on the bar. It skittered along, spotting the tabletop with crimson until it hit an ice bucket. "Probably don't wanna touch that, Sphinx. Tannermann was a real mess by the time we dug it out of him. Still alive enough to beg us not to stick it in his wife, though." He chuckled. "But anyway, you've already got one stuck in yer ass."

Neroy drained his glass and placed it neatly on the counter.

"So," said Dubblz, slouching in his chair. "Enough chit-chat." His eyes went out of focus as he accessed his dataLink. "It's 10 a.m. now, and the job has to happen tomorrow. Sudden opportunity means a tight deadline, but I've nothing to lose—can't say the same for you though. But," he leaned forward and dropped his voice, "there's some good news. Wanna hear it?"

Neroy spread his hands. "I'm a big fan of good news. Until it goes bad."

Dubblz stared at him expectantly. "We've got ourselves a portal generator." Dubblz kept his poker face for a moment, then cackled at Neroy's confusion. Portal generators were enormous things. Huge, Military-Industrial installations, used in offworld mining colonies to create wormholes that shunted ore deposits across vast distances. There were some on Earth, Neroy knew, for dumping toxic waste into the Sun. Stuff like that. But what the hell did that have to do with a bank job?

Dubblz transferred some files to Neroy's dataNode, along with a mass of access codes and encryption keys. The files, whatever was in them, were very heavily protected.

Neroy opened them, then began chuckling as he reviewed the high-level outline. Whatever pressure he was under, at least this part was going to be interesting.

"So what have you got on this Term Tech Professor?" Neroy asked. "Why's he going to let us just borrow the prototype from the University Labs?"

"Ah, the usual sad crap," said Dubblz, swatting at an invisible fly. "Doesn't want his daughter getting her face cut off, you know, shit like that."

"Some people's priorities are just plain distorted, aren't they?" replied Neroy, blinking rapidly as he absorbed the details. "So it's the portable device, right? I can see why it made you want to have a crack at the vault. Something like that's a game changer."

Neroy was no engineer, but the device looked incredible. According to the specification, the portal generator was not only light enough to carry to the location of whatever you needed to move, it didn't require a receiving unit at the other end. You just had to tag the exit point's coordinates, then the generator shunted a pre-defined spatial packet through a quantum tunnel, digging through spacetime with an entangled particle as the drill bit, and spitting out whatever cargo packet the AI had specified at the other end.

The prototype's range was limited to a kilometre, but the potential was incredible.

Neroy was struck by something new in the sea of information. "Hey, says here he's got even smaller units for close-quarters ports. We taking those too?"

The slap from Dubblz came out of nowhere. Neroy rubbed his jaw and blinked away the data overlay.

"Eyes on the prize, idiot!" Dubblz spat. "What's the point of porting something fifty metres? You could just toss it to someone." He leered. "Or stick it up someone's ass. Focus on the prototype, Sphinx. That's got some range. Anyway, the little ones couldn't punch through the Bank's Electronic Warfare shields, they're so weak. Jumps don't even register properly, they decay so quickly."

Neroy wanted another drink, but it wasn't a good idea. "Mind if I ask how you heard about this? Must be one of the biggest tech breakthroughs in years."

"Ah, you know how it is," said Dubblz. "Cops and Feds and the Intelligence Directorate are all too busy screwing each other over to pay attention to the likes of us these days. And they love their informal budget contributions."

"Well, whatever you paid, looks like it was worth it," Neroy said.

"Hell, yeah," said Dubblz. He reached out and yanked on what looked like thin air. The tethered nurse stumbled forwards, and Dubblz splayed his fingers. She began silently cleaning the blood from them with disinfectant gel.

"Yeah," Dubblz continued, watching the nurse. "Guess the last time something radical came onto the market was fully haptic Immersive Reality, thirty years ago now." He snorted. "Bottom fell out of the sex trade, I can tell ya. And before that, anti-grav, I guess."

Neroy felt obliged to engage. "Really? How did anti-gravity affect the sex trade?"

Dubblz scowled. "It didn't, idiot—I was making a, you know, a strategic point. But even that was, what, fifty years ago? I tell you, Sphinx, working stiffs like us? All we get's crumbs from the table."

Dubblz was rambling now, an old man's complaining. Neroy reviewed Dubblz's files again. The generator was clearly a major advance. And based on the background information he was now quickly scanning, Dubblz was right. Breakthroughs like this had become increasingly infrequent in recent decades.

Neroy read on. For the last two centuries, EarthFed's Military-Industrial complex had exploited everything they could find in the Star Systems they'd discovered as they'd expanded through the ancient wormhole network. As they'd explored, Earth humans had found scattered traces of the primordial interstellar civilisation that had used the wormholes before them, aeons ago. Whatever ancient artefacts their survey teams stumbled across were catalogued, analysed and, in a few cases, reverse engineered to produce exotic new technologies far beyond the scope of human science. Portal generators, anti-grav, and a few other isolated wonders. But they were barely understood, hugely complex and incredibly expensive, so in practice such technologies were limited to military and industrial use on Earth, Cassiopia and a handful of advanced worlds. Although now it seemed someone was on the brink of making exotic portals rather more useful.

Unless something unfortunate happened to the prototype.

"Uh, Mr Dubblz, sir?" Neroy offered cautiously. The old man seemed like he was winding down.

"What? What?" barked Dubblz.

"Just for my understanding, sir—why not sell the prototype after we take it?"

"Nah," dismissed Dubblz. He inspected his newly cleaned hands as the nurse packed away her equipment. "Don't have the right contacts for that. All the corporate guys I used to know got downsized years ago. And besides," he shrugged, "I'm traditional. You know. Banks, loot, robberies. Stuff like that." Dubblz tapped his chair controls. It started to rise. "What I need you to do is tell me how it all comes together. Look at the files, use my access codes to get any more information you need, and think things over. No hurry—you've got exactly one hour."

Dubblz clicked his fingers. One of his men lumbered forward. "Why don't you fix Mr Sphinx here a drink? He's dry."

The brothel was a fetish place for metalHedz, people with sexual interests extending to artificial people of all varieties. It worked both ways. Some people wanted to sleep with robots. Others wanted to look like robots themselves when they did it. Or someone did it to them. But this place covered all the angles.

Neroy checked the timeline and sighed. Afternoon already. He'd come up with a plan. Coming up with a plan was never the challenge, though. Just give him a problem the solving of which involved a reversal of someone else's fortune in his direction, and the ideas came from somewhere. Always had. Dubblz hadn't objected to any aspect of it, but the shopping list was extensive and they were already behind schedule, both the one he was pretending to follow, and the one he was actually working to.

Neroy coughed meaningfully at Bigger Guy, who Dubblz had grafted to his side. The meathead dragged himself up from a plush couch and stomped off to find where Madame had disappeared to.

The files and data access rights Dubblz had given Neroy covered his own men, too. About whom Neroy had learned a variety of information that was both prosaic—Bigger Guy's real name was Janks, and Bloody Ear's was Bannax—and sordid—Bannax was having an affair with Janks' ex-wife, which had begun long before she'd left Bigger Guy. Nothing of immediate use there, but worth saving for a rainy day.

The reception lounge was cosy and low lit, everything decked out in shades of pink and crimson. Classic and clichéd, it invoked precisely the atmosphere its clientele demanded. There was a commotion in the office, and a flustered woman stumbled out. She was dressed in a fantasist's idea of an engineer's overalls, her pumped-up physique straining at its tight, revealing lines. Silvery tools bulged out of equipment pouches, many with a gynaecological look.

"Listen, I'm trying to cooperate here," she appealed, as Bigger Guy shoved her along. "Whatever Mr Dubblz wants. But the models you're after, they're very popular! A lot of guys like dressing up as those big, beefy units. I can't just-"

"Let me be direct," said Neroy. "Mr Dubblz, in a circuitous and indirect manner, owns this place. And everything in it. Including you. I don't want anyone to get hurt, but Mr Dubblz needs what he needs. Like, right now."

Bigger Guy backhanded her across the face. She started sobbing.

Neroy jumped up, then checked himself. Nothing to be done about it right now. He picked up his coat and gestured to Bigger Guy to give her space.

"Now, you don't run this place all on your own, do you?" Neroy said. "You have, what, a head of maintenance, something like that, who keeps all the droids and fetish suits running? Right?"

The woman nodded quickly. She gulped, trying not to look behind her at the huge man. "Right. Yes."

"OK. So here's what we're going to do. You tell the maintenance guy to transfer the access codes to my colleague and I. Then you close this place down. Tell your clients there's going to be a police bust in five minutes. Then you're going to give some fetish suits and a droid—the bigger ones, I'm sending you the spec files—to us."

Neroy beamed. "Can you do that?"

Bigger Guy's hand rested on the woman's shoulder. She bit her lip and nodded.

"Perfect," said Neroy. "Let's get to it. My colleague will pick everything up at your loading bay for transfer to our respray place in, oh, ten minutes?"

Bigger Guy headed off to the docking bay, pausing only to flash a small control unit at Neroy and smile. The message was clear. You run, you die. Neroy waited a minute, humming. Then he got the Madame to take him to the medRoom. Place like this was fully stocked for recreational and emergency purposes. Given what some customers liked to do or have done to them, the line between the two was a little blurred, but they had exactly what he needed.

"These should work," sniffed the Madame, handing over the laxative drops, "if you need help with movement."

"Yup," said Neroy. "Movement's what I'm all about."

After the brothel came a trip to Term Tech to extract the prototype from Professor Carver, followed by visits to a range of specialist suppliers across TC. The buzz of it kept Neroy going despite the constant threat. He hadn't chosen the job. Job had chosen him. But he hadn't felt this alive in a long time.

The target bank was their final stop. Posing as a customer, Neroy surreptitiously deployed equipment in a safety deposit room they'd hired. The prowlerWare Dubblz's people were using to subvert the bank's security systems was glitchy, and he ended up having to hurry some of the important stuff, more than he would have had to back in the day. It was all coming back to him, but he felt rusty after years on the shelf. He'd gotten it all done, but now they were late for the briefing.

Neroy felt the acceleration gently push him back in his seat as the shuttle kicked-up a gear. Dubblz had put together a small crew, four freelancers to back up Neroy and Bigger Guy. Their profiles looked okay, although Neroy still needed to run through everything with them in person, iron out any kinks. But they were all on the clock now. The loot was being transferred on to Europa City the next morning.

The nose of the shuttle began to rise into a steeper trajectory. Neroy glanced at Bigger Guy, immersed in course adjustments. They'd been hugging the lower levels so far, TC's older, run-down strata, where it was easy to move unnoticed by law enforcement. But the sacrifice was speed, so the time had come to risk a higher flightpath.

A moment later they were up in the transStream, above the elite-only crests of the tallest structures. From a mile up, the City's scale was brutally apparent. Here in the Core, the enormous dome-topped megaBlocks rippled out in every direction, each one a mini city in its own right, home to tens of thousands. Their dull concrete facades made them look like an undulating desert, riddled with deep fissures formed by the gaps between the blocks, within which shimmering lights formed an endlessly moving haze generated by the transport networks that swarmed each Block, all the way down to the mile-distant ground that lurked below, unseen.

Neroy wrinkled his nose. The lavatorial smell from Bigger Guy was getting really bad. Dubblz was counting on the bomb he'd stuck in Neroy to make him afraid, and obedient. But that act of sadism gave him space to operate, if he could distract his overseer. Dubblz didn't trust anyone, so his employees weren't the smartest. Bigger Guy didn't have much of a clue about Neroy's ostensible plan. But even he would spot blatant divergences. So the laxatives-dropped-in-a-cup-of-coffee-routine had produced a nice little series of timeouts, interludes where Neroy could go off-piste, unobserved.

Term Tech had been the trial run. As soon as Bigger Guy dashed for the facilities, Neroy had gotten Prof Carver to add some Little Extras to the luggageDrone, along with the prototype Dubblz wanted. Even sweetened the deal by giving the Prof a hefty tip—turned out the daughter he was protecting from Dubblz was also prime draft material for TC's depleted, but bribe-hungry, military. Neroy smiled. Bigger Guy had looked mighty pained at such a waste of Dubblz's money. The pattern had continued for the rest of the shopping trip. The guy who'd made the little wooden bird statue for Neroy was a real artist—only took him five minutes to replicate it from the museum catalogue entry. And then the Bank itself. Neroy smirked. Bigger Guy hadn't even made it through the front door, before-

The shuttle jolted onto a different flightpath.

Bigger Guy grunted something as Neroy shifted in his chair. He couldn't really feel the microbomb, but every unexpected jostle brought it to mind. He'd gingerly probed the bomb's codes, but it was secure. Right now, the only way it was coming out was if they decided to remove it. He did have the locateID tag for it now though, ready for later, but that-

The shuttle jolted again, then jerked violently in random directions as though they'd encountered a patch of turbulence. The mouldSeat tightened its grip, holding Neroy in place as the cabin shook. The displays were flashing an unhealthy shade of Alert Red.

"What's happening?" called Neroy. "We OK? I—"

"Trying to dodge a Police patrol that's hailing us," grunted Bigger Guy. "Shuttle's plates ain't registered, but I hoped we'd be OK for a short trip. Just let me-" A proximity alarm screamed into life. Neroy caught a glimpse of black and white as a huge police cruiser dropped in next to them, then emergency restraints popped out of the sides of his chair and enveloped him, pulling him deep into the padding as the seat sunk closer to the floor.

"Shit. Only one way to lose them now. Hold on tight," said Bigger Guy, suddenly enveloped in safety webbing of his own. Neroy looked over just as the man tapped a control tab.

The shuttle's engines died. Their craft dropped out of the sky like it was made of stone.

Secure bioLab facility—Earth

Nassif Taarbeq had been working in the laboratory for three months. That made him the senior member of the dwindling band of technicians, but it didn't count for anything now. Because he hadn't noticed the coolant leak, and now it was too late. They were all going to die, and if they didn't, his employer would likely kill him anyway. This close to probable success, after all the pain and suffering their hideous experiments had caused, her fury would be uncontrollable if he was responsible for frustrating the goal that obsessed her.

He glanced down from his elevated position to the lab space's ground floor. Everyone else was focused on the figure strapped to the surgical table. It was possible he could make it to the airlock before anyone noticed the urgent pulsing of the pressure indicators. Then a swift ascent through the tunnels of Terminus City's sewer system would leave him a short transport ride from Katari, and from there—somewhere else. Anywhere would do.

Taarbeq looked around. The room was dimly lit, illumination mostly coming from the green glow of the nutrient feeds sustaining the pallid human organs in the tanks lining the laboratory's walls, piped in from outside through tubes that snaked around the black metal gantries forming the internal skeleton of the cramped, multi-level workspace. He gathered his courage. A few seconds were all he needed. Best not to delay. There wasn't much time. The indicators were a screeching shade of crimson now.

Nassif rose halfway out of his seat before he realised she was standing behind him.

He stared up into his employer's dead, black eyes. "Th-the coolant pressure. It's spiking. I was just about to-"

Her unwavering glare cut him off. The most unnerving thing about her wasn't her impatient, remorseless certainty. Or the fact that she was glacially beautiful, a towering, blonde Amazonian figure who was at the same time utterly asexual. It was the fact that she never blinked. Her eyes weren't windows into the soul. They were glimpses of an inner void that was profoundly cold and inhuman.

"Hmph." A snort. "You have allowed the coolant to approach a pressure that will result in an imminent explosion. Why?"

"Th-the release valve," Nassif stammered. "It's stuck. I—I didn't notice..."

His employer strode over to the frigid coolant tower. "You are correct. If you had monitored it more closely, you would have been able to reduce the pressure earlier. But now it is peaking too quickly." She rolled up a sleeve of her tight black bodysuit, and removed an access panel. "Immediate action is required."

Nassif edged away. The coolant was minus ninety degrees. His employer inserted her arm, reaching down through the fluid for the emergency release valve. She opened it, and immediately the pressure alert eased off. As her arm withdrew, drops of super-cooled liquid spattered the tower casing, scarring it like acid. Nassif closed his eyes as she strode towards him. The moment drew out, until a rapid clanking on the gantry steps signalled she was descending. He glanced at the nearest control screen. The insertion schedule was still counting down, just minutes to go.

Best look busy.

Nassif's employer was now inspecting the woman strapped to the gurney. Arrayed around the surgical table were a set of articulated cyberArms, loaded with gleaming, bladed instruments. The Arms were stirring in readiness for the procedure, making exploratory stretches and rotations like a cluster of amputated mechanical spider's legs that were probing their environment, in readiness to strike.

Nassif called up a diagnostic for the womb in tank 7G. Everything was optimal. Their procedures never involved anaesthetics. His employer didn't approve of them. So once the instruments had booted up, they were ready to go. Nassif initiated the release protocol for the womb tank. He imagined he could hear the umbilicals detaching, stirring up a surge of bubbles as they withdrew from the pale hunk of human flesh they had sustained for so long.

Then he joined his colleagues below.

His employer looked over as he approached. "The reinforced restraints have now been tested. This procedure will be extremely painful, but any movement will jeopardise the grafting." The woman on the table was staring blankly upwards, breathing slowly. She didn't say anything as the plasBands snapped open, just quickly got down from the gurney and made herself busy at a control station. Nassif's employer climbed onto the table. The restraints closed around her, locking her in place. The womb tank was moved into position. Two Arms with surgical cutting tools unfurled and rotated towards his employer's pelvis, ready for deployment.

A security alert pinged in Nassif's dataLink.

He dearly wanted to ignore it, but it would be much more dangerous for him to interrupt the procedure at a later stage.

"Ahem," he coughed lightly.

His employer couldn't move her head, but she swivelled those black eyes to stare at him. "What is it? We are ready to proceed. Delay at this juncture would be... irritating."

Nassif swiftly got to the point. "Our network's just been scanned. Whoever did it was trying to conceal their identity." He reviewed the incident log. "But they appear to have penetrated quite deeply."

Fenris felt her body strain against the plasBands as she tensed in frustration. She forced herself to relax, then took her dataLink off standby. She reviewed Taarbeq's pathetic update, then compared it to every network security log from the past ten years.

There were several thousand of them, so it took seconds for her to spot the tentative correlation, then cycle the pattern across enough contextual dataSets to be sure. But before she'd completed the procedure, she'd known what she was going to find. A prying intrusion from a former associate. A sanctimonious fool, who spent far too much time concerned with the spiritual welfare of others, and far too little analysing what was really required. An irritating old man, probably still wearing the same white suit he'd had on the last time she'd seen him.

It was Griffin.

Fenris furrowed her brow in irritation. What did he want? And why now? He hadn't been in touch for years. After he'd provided her initial research funding a decade ago, there had been no more direct contact. The occasional errand when his inefficiency required someone with her particular skillset, but those had been infrequent. Thankfully. Her research had been hard enough to conduct as it was, given the constant stupidity of those she was forced to work with.

"Taarbeq," Fenris said. The man's sickly smile popped into her field of vision as he leant over the medical table. "Prepare an updated intelligence report on the Candrassian Order's current activities, specifically related to an Earth-based Elder—one Clarence Griffin. I am sending you some access codes from my personal dataCache." She glared at him. "Use them effectively. I want a full update once the procedure is completed."

Fenris stared up at the surgical lights. This time, she was certain the procedure would succeed. She would move beyond the limits imposed by her creators, finally able to create life of her own. Then the terrible gap in her life would be filled. She would no longer be alone. Fenris closed her eyes and told them to proceed.

The Arms started up with a gentle hum, swiftly overlaid by the high-pitched whine of surgical blades as they approached her skin.

Terminus City, Earth

Neroy's stomach was trying to take up residence in his mouth. The silence was so complete, he could hear the wind rushing past their plummeting craft. Bigger Guy was totally insane. The second the cops had pulled up he'd cut the engines, using thruster bursts to give their freefall a degree of control. But the ground was approaching at terrifying speed.

The shuttle started tipping. A quick thruster blast port side pushed the other way, steadying them. As the shuttle righted itself Neroy caught a flash of green as they streaked past a megaBlock roof garden behind a glass canopy, pleasure lawns tilted at a crazy angle. Then it was gone.

The shuttle rolled again. Through a window now tilted round to what would have been floor level, an island cluster of hovering shops and restaurants rushed up towards them from directly below. He managed half a scream before the thrusters kicked in, smacking the breath out of him. The shuttle blasted forward for a couple of seconds, clear of the floating mall, then the engines cut and they were free-falling past it again. There were fewer craft around them now. The wall of the nearside Block was an ocean of dull concrete peppered

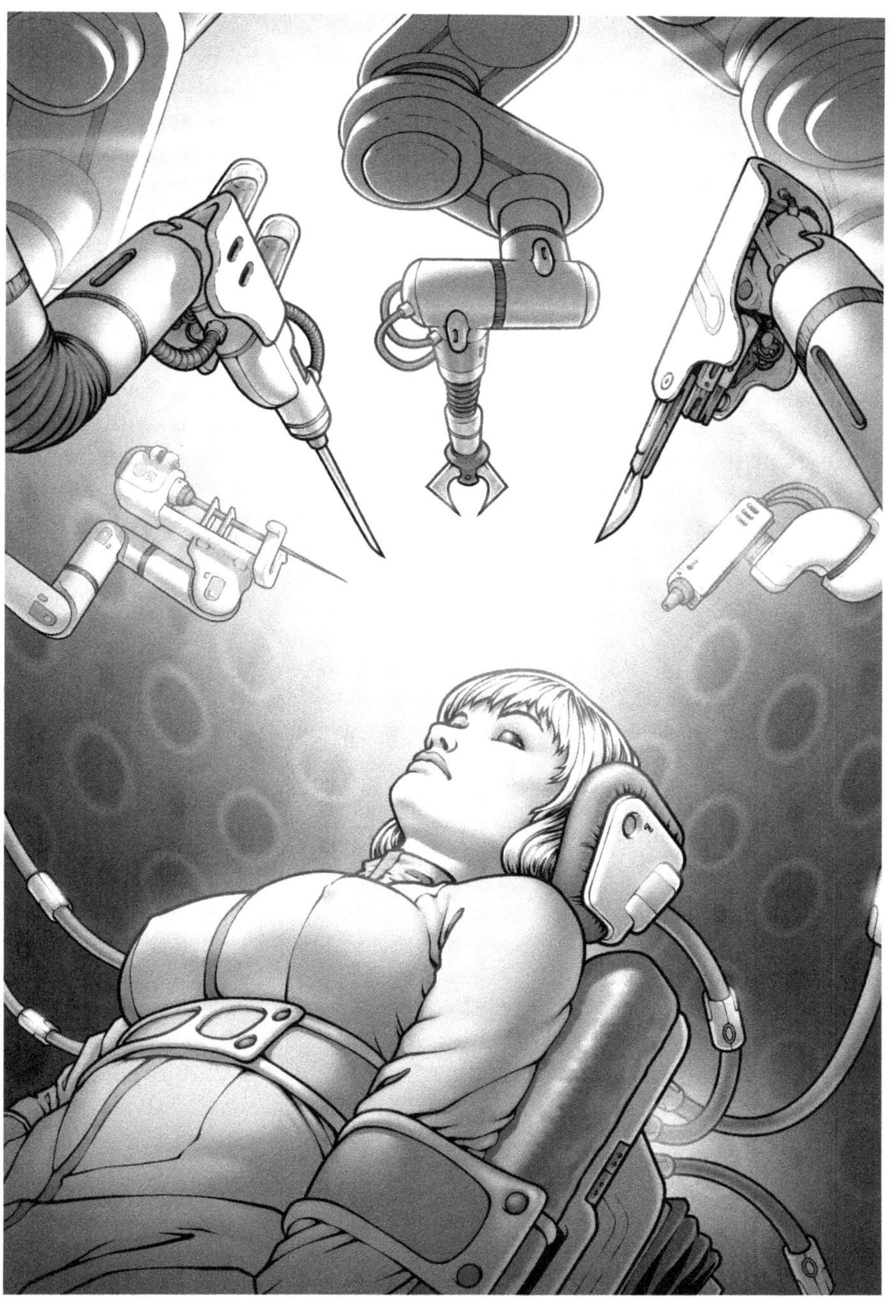

Fenris stared up at the surgical lights.

with apartment windows, residential portholes beyond counting.

Nausea hit. Neroy vomited into his lap, held tight by the chair's snug grip. His dataLink threw a juddering scan of local airspace at him, drawn from the shuttle's sensors. Their stuttering descent vector was plotted messily across it, a suicide-note of a trajectory.

They were tipping backwards now. The thrusters blasted again to switch them into a nose-down angle as they speared through the commercial layer of the Block's local airspace. But the thruster burst hadn't been enough, or Bigger Guy had miscalculated, or something else had gone wrong, because now they were knifing towards two enormous haulage dirigibles.

Neroy screwed his eyes shut, but that did nothing to turn off the data feed, so he saw the shuttle's icon pivot deftly onto its side as he felt the world rotate a full quarter-turn, until the shuttle was flying on one side, presenting the thinnest possible profile to the huge transports shooting up towards them. Another tiny thrust put them dead centre, their line of descent extending through the geometric centre of the dual obstacles. The shuttle icon merged with the dirigibles as the buffeting crosswinds suddenly dropped away. And then they were through, having slid neatly through the narrow gap between the transports.

Lungs bursting, Neroy drew a shuddering breath. The seat webbing tightened to a vice-like grip as the engines turned back on, full-blast, and the shuttle span ninety degrees to end right-side up again as it began clawing itself back to something resembling a powered descent. But their angle was taking them in savagely fast towards a gaping warehouse hangar in the Block's wall.

A transport dirigible was casting off, blocking the hundred-metre hangar entrance. The shuttle's afterburners kicked in as it powered into a controlled turn, curving in way too close to the acres of office-sector window plating surrounding the hangar They screamed past, proximity markers down to under fifty metres.

Then their killer velocity shot them out again, arcing down towards the jumbled knot of expressways that moated the megaBlock's lower reaches.

Bigger Guy slowed down as they arrowed-in closer to the tangle of elevated highways. The expressways seethed with automated vehicles, all tearing along a hair's breadth from each other, skirting the potholes and larger cracks in tightly synchronised swerves. It was late morning, but this far down the megaBlock's shadow created a thick twilight.

The shuttle decelerated as they weaved under the roadways, parallel to the ground. Below was the usual spread of garbage-strewn wasteland, but up ahead a vast underStreet market was swiftly approaching. Like many ground-level areas in the Core, it had a temporary look, but it wasn't going anywhere.

As it blurred past beneath them, Neroy saw the usual collection of canvas stalls, plasBubbles and buildings thrown together from whatever detritus the higher levels of the megaBlock had provided. A tattered commercial shanty town operating in perpetual dusk, crawling with unlicensed vendors, rancid food stalls and customers who couldn't afford anything better. Skimming along a few metres above it, they came to a stop over a cheery cluster of blue-and-white striped tents. It looked like an ancient carnival from a child's picture tablet.

Neroy spat out some vomit and failed to clear his throat. "What's next, friend?" he croaked. "A trip to the goddamn circus? Where-"

The shuttle dropped hard, tearing through canvas and plastic flooring into a dark, cavernous underground space. They finally came to rest on what Neroy hoped was solid ground. Bigger Guy turned the lights off. Neroy sat perfectly still in the darkness, waiting for his heart to slow to something like normal. Exploratory wriggling prompted the seat restraints to loosen a little, and he attempted to clean himself up. But there was nothing he could do about the vile taste in his mouth.

Neroy's dataLink couldn't mesh with anything, but he noticed an ember-like alert icon start pulsing on the main control panel. Then a light stabbed down from far above, and began sweeping from side to side. A searchlight. It seemed a long way off, but the light was sufficient for Neroy to see Bigger Guy's gun come out—and point at him. There was a tremor in the thug's gun hand, with a repeated, artificial pattern to it. For a moment Neroy couldn't be sure, but yes—the man's head was twitching to the same rhythm. Had to be a safety override in his enhancement suite, set up by Dubblz. Bigger Guy wasn't in the driving seat any more. If the cops or whoever it was came much closer, he'd shoot Neroy, then himself. Dubblz' microbomb was just a sadist's toy. Probably wasn't enough to kill him instantly, let alone Bigger Guy.

The search light swept back and forth. It seemed nearer, now.

Neroy strained against the chair, but beyond a certain point he still couldn't move. The restraints were damaged, or Bigger Guy needed to release them. Trapped either way. Claustrophobia kicked in hard. The cityCore extended miles underground in many places, but this forgotten void might as well be at the bottom of the ocean. The darkness was suffocating.

Neroy fought the urge to scream. No one would hear, except possibly the police, which would make things fatally worse. He forced himself to focus on the job, running through every detail of what he'd just done at the Bank.

There hadn't been enough time; that was the problem. He'd used a temporary facial graft to change his appearance, Bigger Guy confined to a bathroom after a laxatives re-up. The respray place had sent one of the brothel droids over, altered to look like a personal bodyguard unit. Also accompanied by a little luggageDrone, he'd then accessed the safety deposit chamber they'd hired, the one he'd told Dubblz was for 'backup equipment'.

Neroy had emptied the luggageDrone, which contained the little wooden statue he'd had made, along with a second disguise and a drink for later on. Plus acid spray to dissolve the ablative surface of the bodyguard droid, revealing the guardDroid design beneath. And finally the Little Extras from Professor Carver. That was when it started to go wrong. He'd reprogrammed the droid and set up the Little Extras with a slaved AI to coordinate it all. But for everything to work, his AI needed to be integrated with the bank's sensor suite.

Dubblz's team had inserted prowlerWare into the bank's network, to corrupt the internal monitors and override the doors and vault locks. But when his AI had sent a passive pre-integration scan, there hadn't been a friendly reply. The bank's systems were proving unexpectedly robust, and the prowlerWare's grip was tenuous. Neroy's AI had cautiously probed a little further, and the situation had looked like it should work out. But it would take hours. Leaving an AI to integrate itself with a partially hostile system wasn't ideal, plus it hadn't scanned his bodily dimensions yet. But he'd had no choice. Assuming it went smoothly, the AI could model his body shape from picking up the positioning of the microbomb later on, and he had the specs for everything else.

So he'd left the AI to itself, and put tracer tags on the robot and wooden statue. That had left the Little Extras. He'd slipped three into his pockets, leaving a fourth on the floor between the statue and the droid. On the way out he'd hidden one at the top of the stairs, in a small alcove behind a trash can. Then-

"Sphinx," came a gravelly whisper.

"Time to go." Bigger Guy tugged off the restraints and Neroy swayed to his feet. He felt a draft from the shuttle's open door. The darkness was disorienting, and he couldn't tell where Bigger Guy was.

Then the smell of recently voided bowels wafted in his direction.

They'd moved on foot through empty subterranean levels until they'd eventually reached the streets, where they'd been picked up by a shuttle identical to the one they'd abandoned. Now they were back at the Academy, but Boss Dubblz wasn't happy. He took Neroy aside on the way to the briefing room, floating his chair in close, his crew keeping a respectful distance.

"I heard about you paying the Prof," Dubblz began. "You actually trying to rile a man who's holding the detonator to a bomb in yer ass?"

Neroy shrugged. He wasn't sure where Dubblz was going with this one.

"You've changed, Sphinx," Dubblz continued. "You know that voice we all have inside that says, *"ah, screw it, I better not do it—it ain't worth it?"* You don't seem to have that so much no more. Not compared to how you were back in the day, anyways." Dubblz tilted his head and stared at Neroy with suspicious curiosity. "It ain't natural, ya weirdo."

Neroy felt it wiser to let Dubblz carry on. It seemed he had more to say. But Dubblz was right. Sometimes the fun and games were all that mattered, when your blood was up. Go ahead, roll the dice, and let them catch you if they could.

"Another thing," Dubblz continued, slightly concerned. "You seem a little, I dunno—little less of an asshole. Little less cold, little more, ah... a little more *emotional.*" Dubblz glared at Neroy, then thumbed a control. His chair started drifting away. "It better not impact your performance, Sphinx." Dubblz floated off down the corridor, his tethered nurse stumbling after.

A crew of four waited in the briefing room. They were a raggedy bunch, wearing aggressive City fashions. Leather jackets, torn clothes and big boots, all of them festooned with spikes, kneepads, facial piercings and fluorescent hair spikes.

Neroy perched on the edge of a table and lit up. "It's been need to know so far, but now you're in the bubble, you'll get the files and schematics in a minute. But first, let me tell you how it's going to go down."

He smiled. Moments like this, life felt like it all made sense. "Now, regulations say that all subterranean vaults need manually accessible tunnels, to stop people getting trapped. City Security's stretched thin these days, so the design work for the last upgrade of the Bank's security systems was contracted out. Naturally the cops oversaw the work, but the force ain't what it used to be." Neroy took a drag on his smoke. "Anyway, suffice it to say we can access the vault. Problem lies in getting out again. There's a huge amount of loot, but those tubes are strictly crawl space only, and we can't cut all the alarms. That's where part two comes in. Now, we happen to have access to a mobile portal unit they've been developing at Term Tech."

His dataLink sent them the specs. He gave them a little while to scan the details, then the muttering began. He raised his voice. "I know, I know—soon as we use it, City Security will have a fix on our location and they'll trace the port signal in seconds—a minute at most. Wherever we go. But that's all we'll need—to leave with the loot ourselves. Now, there's limited room in the access tunnel, but there is enough space for us to wear our droid outfits right from the start."

Four brows furrowed at that one.

Neroy chuckled. "That's right—droid outfits. Robot costumes. Straight from a metalHedz brothel. Don't worry," he said, raising his hands, "they've been thoroughly disinfected."

He made a mental note to add a digital tag to Bigger Guy's droid suit, so the Bank's sensors could distinguish it from the others. "So. Once we're in, we'll go straight to the engineering bay and take out the real security droids. We've been infiltrating the bank's systems for twenty-four hours now with prowlerWare. So we can temporarily override security inside the place, but that's no use if we get nabbed in thirty seconds once we step outside. So we'll set a timer to port out the resulting junk from the droids we blast, and we'll pick up the loot ourselves. Half a dozen crates, one for each of us, and we'll walk out the front door with it, just as the 'port happens. We're creating a fake interbranch transfer for some low-level assets, scheduled for just then. When we crash the internal systems, we'll just be a bunch of droids doing a regular transport run amongst all the confusion."

Neroy blinked. He also needed to calibrate the exoskeleton boosters on the droid suits so they were less sensitive. That way, the crew shouldn't notice the sudden shift in weight when the cascade happened.

A young woman at the front of the room frowned. "So the cops are just gonna let us walk out with it all? Is that really gonna work?"

Neroy stifled a sneer. Time to dumb it down. "OK. We sneak in disguised as security droids. We shoot the real security droids, making a big pile of junk. Our prowlerWare lets us access the vault, but as soon as we do it triggers an external alarm for the cops that we can't stop."

He paused to check the woman looked happier. Good. She was nodding along. "We use the portal generator to beam out the robot junk as a decoy when we walk out the door disguised as bank droids, carrying the loot. The cops divert from storming the bank to chase the portal signal, thinking we're escaping that way—but all they find is junk. And by then, we're gone."

He couldn't stop himself grinning. The little blue bird statue shouldn't get picked up by the Bank's door scanners at all. It was the only wooden piece in the whole collection. "Simple misdirection."

Boss Dubblz watched them as they got ready to board the shuttle, looking for all the world like six bank security droids with oddly-human body language. Sphinx had assured him the servo motors in the suits would disguise that once the job began, and he had no reason to doubt it. Sphinx had proved to be nothing but competent so far.

A pity they wouldn't be working together again.

Dubblz pinged his enforcer's dataLink with the kill order as they started lumbering up the shuttle ramp. Some of them, like the woman, had needed layers of extra cushioning inside to pad the metal outfits. But the droid suit had barely accommodated his guy's massive frame. Sphinx would get them in there, and Sphinx would get them out again.

Dubblz smiled. And as soon as they got back, he was a dead man.

The access tube was a cramped, dark tunnel cutting deep underground at a sharply sloping angle. They'd only been inside for a minute, but already Neroy felt claustrophobia closing in. The suit was stifling. The discomfort had been OK when they were outside, but they were packed so tightly inside the tube he felt like he couldn't breathe. A rough patch on the torso plate was beginning to scrape his chest, and sweat was stinging his eyes. Neroy was in the middle of the group, two ahead and three behind. If anything happened, he wouldn't be able to move. He'd be wedged tight, trapped inside a metal suit inside an underground tunnel, waiting for the air to run out.

A burst of static sounded over the audio channel. "Heads up," came Bigger Guy's voice. He was on point up ahead. "I'm coming out in the sub-basement."

Seconds later, Neroy felt the floor levelling off. He waited for the people ahead of him to shuffle forward then clanged out into a murky chamber, dark aside from some weakly glowing power indicators. He switched to infrared. It was a bare synthiCrete room lined with energy conduits and cabling, some of which disappeared back up the tunnel they'd just descended.

The tactical overlay sprang up in his visor as he moved away from the rest of the crew towards the far wall. He ran an armoured hand over it, feeling nothing. It was completely featureless, but it was the one they wanted. The door leading out of the room was behind him, but that would only take them up to the staffroom, and the reception area above it.

Neroy activated his suit mic. "OK, guys, this is it. Security droids are on the other side of this wall in the engineering bay. Our prowlerWare's compromised their repair cycle, brought them all there and powered them down. Should have cut the sensor feeds to the wall, too. And the human staff are all outside—we just set off a fire alarm."

He reviewed the latest update from the prowlerWare. It could only send data packets during a safe window, but everything had been on schedule as of fifteen minutes ago. "So let's do it."

Neroy joined the crew as Bigger Guy stomped up to the wall. He checked his suit diagnostics while Bigger Guy's weapons systems powered up. Everything was optimal. They all had blasters in their gauntlets, like the real guardDroids did. But Bigger Guy's had been souped-up to give them the kinetic punch required to knock through the wall without any messing.

A pale lilac energy signature was building-up around Bigger Guy's armoured hands, raised now to point towards the wall, fingers outstretched as though poised to dive straight through it. The glow grew more intense. Then it screamed up through the visual spectrum to become a shocking, sun-like blaze that seared into the wall in a stream of crackling energy. One second the wall was there, the next a large circle had been surgically removed from it.

A roomful of active guardDroids turned to face them, weapons powering up.

Neroy put his suit into reverse and shuffled behind the rest of the crew. His gauntlet blasters activated. The guardDroids were killEnabled units, but they still had hard coded safety protocols, so they weren't going to shoot first. Neroy activated his mic. "OK, listen up. Droids are still active, so the prowlerWare's obviously glitching. But we just need to-"

The guy in front of him tore open as a laz-beam stabbed through the hole in the wall. The man slammed back into Neroy, knocking him to the floor. A ragged chunk was missing from the man's torso. The weight of the dead man's suit pinned Neroy to the ground as the air erupted in a hissing crossfire of energy discharges. The remaining crew scrabbled away, pumping blaster fire back through the hole. A fusillade of laz-beams slammed into the wall over Neroy's head, vaporising the tangled power cables in a spray of molten plastic. He cursed the prowlerWare. Must have come up against something sticky in the droids' systems.

Neroy flinched as part of the wall crashed down onto his legs. He sucked in a lungful of stale air and forced his mind back to the plan. The droids were where they were supposed to be. It could still work. Neroy blinked hard, and turned off the infrared. There were so many energy discharges he couldn't make anything out. He wanted to fire back, but was still trapped under the armoured corpse. Neroy activated his suit's servomotors and rose onto his elbow, then rotated to face in the right direction.

A squall of feedback scoured the audio channel "-inished re-charging, but I need some goddamn cover!" screamed Bigger Guy. "Go for a burst on my mark!"

Neroy twisted his helmet round as far as he could. Bigger Guy was edging along the wall, heading towards the hole, a pulsing lilac glow building up around his gauntlets. Shadows clumsily re-positioned around the chamber's edges as the crew momentarily stopped firing. The laz-fire from the guards dropped away too.

Neroy picked up movement through the hole. The guardDroids were advancing. At a shout from Bigger Guy the crew started pumping blaster fire at them. He yelled orders over the audio circuit, and the crew's barrage slowly moved away from the right-hand edge of the circular hole, drawing the droids" return fire with it, to create an open position.

Bigger Guy stepped out from behind the curving rim of synthiCrete and raised his arms towards the droids. Twin streams of blazing light erupted from his gauntlets, but not at the same shockingly intense level as before. His torso slowly rotated from left to right and back again as he scoured the engineering bay with a stream of pulverising energy. Then the discharge ceased, and everything was darkness.

Neroy turned his infrared back on. Bigger Guy had disappeared into the next room. For a moment there was silence, then a crackling invitation came.

"OK, we're good. Let's move it, people."

The engineering bay was a cybernetic abattoir. Droid debris and partially melted equipment littered the floor in a steaming drift of wreckage. It crunched satisfyingly underfoot as Neroy stomped through it.

Inside his helmet, he smiled. It was perfect.

Bigger Guy set down the portal prototype he'd been carrying in the middle of the room, then led the rest of the crew to the vault, one level up. Neroy stayed behind. He checked his suit chronograph: 19:17:02. He set the timer for exactly five minutes. The capture radius was two metres. That should shift enough droid wreckage to correspond to the total mass of the loot the five remaining crewmembers could carry. Or so the AI modelling said. He checked the door, then slipped one of the Little Extras he'd taken from Prof Carver inside a pile of wreckage near the wall.

The crew were waiting outside the massive vault door when he caught up with them. He sent an initiate code to the prowlerWare and licked his lips. Now came the tricky part. Ultimately, it was a question of balancing competing outcomes. On the one hand, crash the remaining bank systems and use Dubblz's override codes to open the vault. On the other, leave the bank's internal sensors functioning on skeleton mode, giving his AI in the safety deposit room something to piggyback off so it could manage the cascade later on.

Slowly, the colossal vault door slid open. Neroy's dataLink pinged a tactical alert. The external police alarms had always been beyond their control, and they'd just been triggered by the unscheduled vault opening. But the cops would be coming in dark, as the surveillance system had just crashed. All part of the plan.

Neroy uploaded a batch command to the crew's personal network. Their suits clanged into the vault in jerky, quickened motions as their guidance systems took over, coordinating their movements and speeding everything up. They had five minutes to get it done if they were going to sync their exit with the portal timer. The loot awaited in huge transfer crates in a caged area within the vault. Neroy took point as Bigger Guy wrenched the metal door open. He strode past Bigger Guy into the cage, throwing a direct message at him on a closed channel to watch their backs while he confirmed the payload.

Neroy waited until Bigger Guy turned around, then sprayed tracer tags on five of the boxes before prising Crate #2 open. He smiled. The manifest hadn't led him astray. There at the top, swathed in shockGel, was a small wooden statue of a blue bird. He dropped in the final Little Extra from Prof Carver, then sprayed a tracer tag on the statue.

See you soon, little birdie.

Three minutes later they were at the top of the stairs at ground floor level, five metallic figures carrying sturdy crates, stomping in unison towards reception. Forty-eight seconds until portal initiation. Everything was set up. Everything was rolling. Neroy visualised it like a circuit diagram, with each component set up to swap places in a clockwork cascade once he flipped the switch. He felt giddy, terrified it would fall apart while knowing it wouldn't.

Best feeling in the world.

The doors to the foyer were coming up. Beyond them lay the main entrance. Just one last piece to slot into place now. Himself. Neroy checked the timeline, then loaded a fake alert into the crew's network. At least he could take advantage of all the prowlerWare glitches now.

He messaged Bigger Guy, injecting panic into his voice. "Signal from the portal unit's dropping out—timer's malfunctioning. Must be the prowlerWare screwing up again!"

Bigger Guy's droid suit kept clomping forward, but he replied instantly. "Fix it, Sphinx—now!"

Neroy unhooked his suit's guidance system and pivoted in a quick 180, back towards the vault. "On it—there's a data node I can access at the top of the stairs!"

He reached the alcove in seconds. Shifting his stance to grip the crate one-handed, he gave the trash can a little pat. Prof Carver's Little Extra was wedged in nice and tight behind it, where he'd stashed it earlier. Neroy brought up the timeline for a final check: 19:17:57. Five seconds to the main port at 19:22:02. Perfect timing. Neroy smiled. He imagined a good old-fashioned red button being pressed as he sent the trigger signal to start the cascade, and-

Boss Dubblz was so excited he'd untethered his nurse for the evening, then cleared out the hangers-on who usually propped up the bar in the Academy sub-basement at a time like this. Good news, a rich haul, and suddenly everyone wanted to join the party. Well, screw that. He didn't need any distractions. His

men had picked the crew up after they'd dumped the stolen security shuttle, and they'd just landed outside. Wouldn't be long now. Dubblz floated his chair down and eased himself out, stretching his aching back. Haul like this, he could buy himself a new goddamn back.

Maybe he could re-use some of Sphinx's, after they'd finished dissecting him. He smirked. His men were busy cleaning Tannermann's remains away right now, getting things nice and ready for the next guy.

A metallic tramping became audible, each step falling in perfect synchronisation. Still using their guidance systems to automate their movements, still in character throughout the journey back, in case they ran into any patrols. Home free now, but still. He'd wanted to see how it looked.

Dubblz rubbed his hands as the five of them trooped in, each carrying a hefty transfer crate. They formed a straight line in front of him, soldiers on parade. It was better like this, he mused. No one to talk back, for a start. Dubblz shuffled forward and patted one of them on the shoulder.

"Well done boys, well done! Let's see what we got here." He got them to line the crates up on the floor and loosen the lids. Anticipation was everything with something like this. Dubblz circled the boxes, stopping at the one in the middle. Gently, he lifted the cover free.

His hands shook, lid clattering to the floor.

The look on his face was one of utter surprise. Slowly, he reached into the crate and drew out a fragment of blasted metal. Scorched and heat-blackened, but a logo was still legible: *SECURITY.* The crate was full of broken droid parts. Dubblz yanked the lids off the other boxes. All the same.

He screamed. "Sphinx! Sphinx! Where are you?!" Dubblz hurled the metal plate at the nearest droid. "Take off those frickin' helmets, you idiots!"

Seconds later, Bigger Guy and the three surviving freelancers were staring at the fifth member of their crew. Ordered by Dubblz to remove its helmet, the droid had complied as best it could by opening the inspection plate on the side of its head.

"Sphinx! I want him dead—now!" Dubblz' face was a deep shade of crimson.

Bigger Guy opened a compartment in his suit's torso and took out the microbomb's control unit. Dubblz snatched it from him and stabbed at the control tab. A tiny sliver of time passed, enough to hear an almost inaudible *klikt.*

Bigger Guy's hand exploded, covering Dubblz with a spray of scarlet gore.

Neroy tossed the empty Citi Ade drink carton into the corner of the bank's safety deposit room. An hour had passed. Time to move. The prowlerWare had suicided as soon as the crew left the building, scouring every trace of itself from the bank's systems. But the AI he'd been using to run the portal cascade and then maintain a sensor bubble around him was a separate system, and he could risk a passive scan now the main police sweep of the bank's network had cycled through.

Neroy brought up the system logs for the small portal units, the Little Extras he'd obtained from Professor Carver along with the main prototype, when Bigger Guy had been indisposed in the Professor's bathroom. The small units were only good for close-quarters ports, like Dubblz had said. But sometimes close-quarters was all you needed. According to the logs, the cascade had manifested exactly as intended, the AI using the tracer tags he'd hidden to model the transit sequences and displacement volumes like clockwork:

>>

[19:22:01:00] The loot had ported from the stolen crates the crew were carrying, back into the vaults...

[19:22:01:01] ...replaced by five equivalent packets of droid wreckage from the engineering bay...

[19:22:01:02] ...the antique wooden bird statue from the loot had been swapped with the fake one he'd had made, and then left in the deposit room...

[19:22:01:03] ...the microbomb had been ported from his ass direct into Bigger Guy's hand...

[19:22:01:04] ...and he'd swapped himself and his droid suit with the robot stored in the deposit room, that was programmed to hurry after Bigger Guy and return to Dubblz...

[19:22:02:00] ...followed by the main port itself, dumping a circular slice of engineering bay wreckage in a local warehouse for the cops to puzzle over.

<<

Neroy scanned the passive survey results. As far as the authorities were concerned, nothing had been stolen. The loot was all back in the vault. All that was missing were five worthless transfer crates, and some of the shattered remains of the bank's guardDroids. No cops were currently on site, and the bank staff were clearing up the lower levels, waiting for an ambulance to take away the armoured corpse from the chamber next to the engineering bay.

He quickly layered on the disguise he'd prepared. Wouldn't pass a close inspection, but he looked close enough to one of the bank staff he'd selected that he should be able to leave unchallenged. Neroy set the AI to suicide itself and picked up the little blue bird. The only wooden piece in the collection, included on some curator's whim. And the only item the bank's scanners couldn't detect when he walked out the door. He never had understood art, but it was a cute little fellow.

Neroy put it in his pocket and left.

Something about the cocktail the woman next to him was drinking bothered Neroy, but he didn't know why. Then he realised. It was the same shade of pink as whatever by-product of Tannermann's torture had ended up on Boss Dubblz's slippers yesterday. Neroy moved to an empty gelCouch facing the door and checked his dataLink again. Nothing. Leonard, the fence he'd arranged to meet to offload the statue, was seriously late. If his contacts weren't fifteen years out of date, he wouldn't have been forced to take a chance on someone he didn't know. But there was nothing he could do about it now.

Neroy sipped his Cosmo and scanned the dingy bar.

Nothing out of place amongst the flickering holoScreens and murmuring conversations. But it wouldn't pay to hang around until something was. Five minutes. No more. This was the worst part of a job, when you just had to wait for someone else to come through.

He drummed his fingers on the armrest, then threw back his drink. No time for another. Neroy sank deep into the couch, relaxing his shoulders. Staring at the door made him feel jumpy, so he wrenched his thoughts away from the here and now. Nothing else had come back over the last couple of days concerning his missing years. The Cold Black Glass was still just sitting there. Nothing special had occurred to him from before the start of the memory gap either, no clue as to where the Glass had come from. He'd just been doing a job, holed up in some bland-but-opulent hotel.

But then, on the other side of the Glass where his memories resumed, a name suddenly resolved out of the dim memory of an icy, faraway place that had been in the back of his skull since yesterday, when he'd first recalled it whilst sitting at Dubblz's bar.

Kumeiijm'a.

A quick dataLink search produced images of some obscure iceball planet. But that was definitely it—the first place he remembered being after the gap. Seeing it brought back more. The details were sharper than the Peach Heights years, like whatever lay behind the Cold Black Glass had flared briefly back to life on Kumeiijm'a, before guttering and dying for the next decade. He'd been on a job. With a woman in black. A very unusual, very tall, blonde woman. Just before Peach Heights, but lightyears away.

And it was exactly when EarthFed had fallen apart.

Was there a connection? He tried pushing back further, but his head throbbed. He pushed again, but the pain worsened and-

A ping on his dataLink from Leonard, the fence, hauled Neroy back from the edge of the Black Glass. He shook his head, grateful for the interruption.

Neroy met Leonard in a loading bay. Then, newly solvent from selling the priceless little bird statue, he headed for Katari Spaceport. Dubblz wasn't going to stop looking for him, which left one direction of travel. Katari was a small city in its own right. Even in these straitened times thousands poured through it every day, channelled through a sprawl of shopping malls, hotels and warehouses arranged in ragged concentric circles around the gleaming tower, cable-thin in places, that stretched up to Earth's Orbital Hub, a hundred kilometres above.

From the Orbital, interSystem craft ferried passengers to and from Sol's Gateway, deep in the gravitational calm of Earth's second Lagrange Point, and from there—onwards, out through the branches of the interstellar wormhole network to Star Systems in their hundreds. Neroy took a circuitous route, spiralling in slowly in the wake of an advance frontier of sweeper software he'd cloned from the stuff Dubblz had paid for. But nobody seemed to be waiting for him.

He chose a shabby lounge for commercial travellers and booked a departure slot on the Orbital Elevator. A mart was selling personal equipment for offworld environments. Neroy picked up a breather helmet, his distorted reflection looking back at him from the curving faceplate. He hung it back up, next to a motionPoster of some rugged exoplanet, and smiled. Long before places like Katari actually existed people had imagined what they'd be like, envisaging Spaceports with little green men amongst the human travellers. But the only aliens mankind had ever encountered were a bunch of mindless wildlife. Early explorers from Earth had always had expectations, and every now and then an exoplanet had been discovered where humanity had evolved far enough from the baseline that they initially seemed alien. But they never were.

The rest of the human race always seemed disappointed when that happened. To be left alone with the wildlife. Neroy walked past a motionPoster of a tumbling Altarian FurCub. Some of that wildlife was pretty damn cute, though.

A nudge from his ticketID told Neroy his ride was coming up. The problem

was where to go. He could buy a flight anywhere. But he had to choose quick, and it had to be right.

Kumeiijm'a was one possible destination, but he had to assume now that whatever had happened to him was somehow tied up with The Fall. That something had been done to him, that it wasn't just some illness or accident. And whoever had done it might be coming back for another bite. So there was more stuff to keep ahead of than just Dubblz. And Kumeiijm'a might be a little too much of a dead-end if someone came calling.

Lots of flights tonight. Altraxia, Sirius, Barnard's Star. Problem was, information on potential destinations was patchy these days. Since The Fall, extrasolar travel had become harder and much more expensive—a commercial, military, elite occupation. Interstellar holidays for the masses were long gone. And a prolonged interplanetary depression had kicked advertising out from underneath the media houses, so no more expensive news packages were shared between Systems.

Simultaneously, barriers had gone up everywhere from suspicious System governments. Trading data and military intelligence were shared between allies. But facts on the ground were out of date, provincial and sparse, driven by the agenda of whoever happened to have uploaded the latest information batch onto a particular star ship.

Neroy grimaced. A bunch of destinations, but no way to be sure exactly what was going on in any of them. A brewing war or a nasty pandemic was the last thing he wanted to stumble into.

The reminderPulse was becoming insistent. Neroy headed for the barriers. He'd avoid backwater Systems, getting painted-in. That ruled a lot of places out. There were roughly two hundred inhabited human planets. The wormhole system was complex and fragmented, so some places were easy to reach, with others taking longer. Point-to-point travel wasn't always possible. A few Systems had two wormholes, and transfers from one sub-branch to another were occasionally required. Some worlds were distant from their System's wormhole, further increasing transit times.

Added to this, for reasons dimly understood, not all journeys took an equal time. Some point-to-points were instantaneous. But others took hours or days. A few lasted weeks. Earth had the good fortune to be at the centre of the system, in terms of access to useful main routes to other important worlds. But many planets were isolated.

Tonight's flight schedules gave Neroy a good spread of options. Core Worlds, Independent Systems, Earth Colonies. The luxury of the Inner Systems was tempting. Cassiopia, the jewel in the crown, was a single transfer away. He could be there tomorrow, living it up with a bevy of the clone girls for which the place was infamous.

...but no.

Something had awoken in him after a long sleep. Something he wanted to ride a little more. Perhaps it would be best to stay away from the centre of things, for a while. Off the grid. A little exploration around the rough edges first. Proxima would do. It had been on the edge of becoming unmanageably wild last time he'd been there, but it was a transport hub, and there was a flight in two hours. That should buy him time to think, start figuring out what had happened to him, in a place no one would be looking for him. So not Kumeiijm'a. Not yet. That far out on the rim, you'd really have your back to the wall if things went south. Best do some limbering up first. Get fighting fit.

The ticket cost half his money, but that still left a nice pile once he was through the scanBarrier. More than enough to live in comfort for a while. Deep fatigue seeped in from the edges as he fell into a departure-lounge bubbleChair. He'd made it. Back in the game. His eyes drooped, but on the edge of sleep a golden shimmer snagged his attention. The cheery holoScreens of a casino were beckoning from across the lounge.

Neroy sauntered over, whistling a shapeless tune. There was half an hour to kill. It would be a terrible shame to waste it.

CHAPTER 4: INTERSTITIAL

Candrassian Order Mother Temple, Earth

The central Cloister Nest was Griffin's favourite. It was the largest in the Temple, containing the small rose garden where he was currently sitting, awaiting news from the messenger slowly descending the access ramp. He considered Acolyte Lamai as she approached. A young woman with tawny skin and a severe black bob, she had a pleasing seriousness.

"Greetings, my dear," he smiled. "Please, join me."

Griffin glanced at the Nest's display case as she sat. It contained a partially melted object that evoked the look of a human face, despite its profoundly non-human lines. Lamai followed his gaze, then looked at him with a hint of accusation.

"Is it still safe for those things to be on display, sir?"

Griffin stared at her. "Those 'things' are holy artefacts, Acolyte. Capable of generating powerful Visions amongst sensitives. Especially so given recent developments in... celestial circumstances. Fortunately, I am able to control the physical impact of any such revelations."

He grimaced. They'd had to amputate Fajid's leg due to blood loss. And one

"Greetings my dear. Come join me."

of her arms. "How is Brother Azrael, by the way?" The night before, the strain of Griffin's Gifting had finally overwhelmed the poor man. He had attempted to gouge out his eyes. It was all most regrettable.

Acolyte Lamai made a face. "Heavily sedated. The surgeons may be able to save his sight, but it's too early to tell."

"...ah," Griffin responded. "I see," he said, immediately wincing at his choice of words. Azrael's condition was deeply unfortunate. Griffin had been counting on his operational support. He himself lacked the time for administrative matters.

"If I may ask, sir, what was the nature of your vision?" Lamai leaned in. "As Brother Azrael's understudy, I am aware of some of what is occurring, but..."

Griffin nodded sagely as he suppressed a surge of fear. "A terrible evil has awakened. One that threatens us all. For now, it lurks on the other side of the galaxy. But surrounding it, dark shapes flitter like hungry arrowheads, sniffing at our scent, even now turning towards us…"

Lamai gasped. "What is this evil, sir? What form does it take?"

Griffin thought of Azrael. "Ah, the precise details need not concern us." He shivered. The Fajid Vision had been profoundly disturbing. He had always hoped they would have more time. "However. Have there been reports of anything... unusual arriving in the Kumeiijm'a System lately?

"Unusual, sir?"

"Visitors of an unexpected nature, perhaps? If you'd kindly use that wonderful dataLink of yours to liaise with our military contacts, I would be deeply appreciative."

Lamai's eyelids flickered. Seconds passed, then stretched out. Griffin felt himself becoming impatient. It had been a mistake to allow himself to become distracted by her talk of his Vision. Lamai had likely arrived with the update on Sphinx he'd requested. Suddenly desperate for information, Griffin considered reading her mind. But no. There was decorum to follow. And psychic probes and dataLinks didn't mix well.

Sphinx was supposed to have remained in hospital until the Order retrieved him. But his instincts had evidently re-emerged more quickly than anticipated. After he'd discharged himself, they'd lost track of him in the City underworld. Although police contacts were now tying Sphinx to a bank robbery that had occurred some days ago. It was all most unexpected.

The flash of Insight came upon him unbidden, as they sometimes did. A Vision of the future—in this case, someone else's, rather than his own—coming from out of nowhere, a premonition momentarily overlaying the physical world. A dream made solid. Griffin focused on what details he could. A man, falling from the sky of an alien world towards... a mountain of excrement. His lip curled. He could almost smell it. But the man. There was something familiar about him. Could it-

The Vision shimmered, and was gone. Lamai was still interfacing, but clearly about to surface.

"There's nothing happening in the Kumeiijm'a System our sources are aware of, sir," Lamai reported, once she had snapped back to her surroundings. "At least not as of eighteen hours ago. That's... the, er, most recent data... available..." Lamai drifted to a distracted conclusion. Griffin pursed his lips. She hadn't registered on the Order's psychic aptitude tests, but perhaps external circumstances were stimulating a latent capability. It wasn't unknown.

If so, she needed to retreat from any proximity to the artefacts. Immediately.

Dark sunspots of exotic matter manifested around Griffin's hands, ready to channel his abilities should an urgent tactical application be required. The black globules quivered hungrily in the air, as though eager to be released.

Then Griffin saw what was diverting Lamai. He relaxed, the sunspots winking out of existence.

The Cloister Nest was atypical. It was the only Nest with a garden, and the only one with a bar. It was also the only Nest with a Custodian, tending to both flowers and patrons. Taking advantage of a quiet moment, the Custodian was pruning a nearby rose bush. The skeletally-thin figure wore a Senior Acolyte's grey jerkin and leggings, but their face and hands were completely covered by bandage-like wrappings. With a firm snip they deadheaded a white rose, then ran their fingers in a lingering sweep down the wicked blade of their secateurs.

Griffin nodded to them, responding to an unspoken question. "Tea would be lovely, thank you." He smiled at Lamai. "Anything for you, my dear, before we address the reason for your visit?"

Lamai wrenched her attention back. "No, I'm fine, sir," she replied. "Apologies for my lack of focus." Griffin gestured for her to continue. "Our people at Katari have been keeping an eye out for Sphinx," Lamai began, "as you directed. They've picked up his trail. He boarded a ship for Proxima. After apparently becoming involved in some kind of incident at a casino, but details are unclear."

Griffin's brow knitted. "Proxima. Hmm. Well, that isn't necessarily a disaster." The intention had been for a sedated Sphinx to be shipped offworld to the high-tech affluence of Cassiopia, directly from the hospital. For a sheltered recuperation, with the cognitively-oriented medtech of Cassiopia, the best in The Systems, available as a contingency against any unexpected medical developments. During which time he would become the sharp, effective instrument the situation demanded.

"Instructions, sir?"

Griffin folded his hands in his lap. "Sphinx must be shepherded onwards, to Cassiopia. The Order has an excellent sanatorium there, necessary for the final phase." And there was something else in the Cassiopia System. A small expeditionary fleet was assembling with the tacit support of sympathisers within the Cassiopian government, away from the eyes of a paranoid Earth, to transport them through the Great Arterial Link. With Sphinx at his side. "But it won't be easy," Griffin sighed. "Proxima is unfortunately a rather hostile place for members of our Order. However, Sphinx's recovery is vital for us all."

Lamai drew herself up. "I would be honoured to participate, sir. To continue the work of my mentor at this critical time."

Griffin nodded. "Thank you, my dear. It will be dangerous, but your familiarity with the situation makes the case for your involvement. However, you must act within a team of our most experienced operatives."

A waft of jasmine preceded the arrival of a pot of gently steaming tea. Griffin raised his cup.

"To the success of your mission, Acolyte—Proxima awaits!"

CHAPTER 5: CAUGHT INTRIGUE

De'Spyr, Mu Draconis System

Neroy had almost made it to the docking bay when the alarms started up with a throbbing howl. He thought he'd taken out the surveillance systems on this deck of the ship before abandoning his bolthole, but he must have missed something. Neroy jumped down a metal stairway and sprinted along the corridor. Felt like his heart was about to explode.

A stretch of grey composite wall blurred past as he ran for the bay. Inside it was a basic one-man craft. Little more than a missile with life support, it was also a quickLaunch, and that was all that mattered. Neroy paused at the bulkhead door. Chest heaving, he scanned the docking bay. The Launch had an aggressively skeletal design, all struts and support beams, its cladding striped in waspish yellow-and-black. The umbilicals were detached, cockpit cracked open.

Neroy checked behind him. It was too easy.

The traders just weren't that well-organised. The ship was a mess, a barely spaceworthy hodgepodge of jury-rigged equipment from dozens of different systems, constantly on the edge of a catastrophic breakdown. Neroy looked around the corridor. Someone had removed a wall panel to carry out repairs and hadn't put it back. He tossed it through the doorway.

The metal door petals irised shut in a blur of motion, slicing the panel in half. The alarm cut off mid-howl. Neroy heard footsteps pummelling down the stairs from the upper levels. Which left only one option.

An airlock.

The main one on this level was back behind him, but the crew were coming from there, so that left the starboard portal. Neroy pelted down the passageway and up a ramp to the secondary cargo bay, a beaten-up metal chamber crammed with unsold trade goods. Grunting, he pushed a couple of heavy cases in front of the door and hurried to the airlock. Seldom used, there were no suits or breathers in the lockers.

Hammering erupted behind him. The boxes blocking the door slid a little. He had a few seconds, no more. Neroy scanned the room. Nothing visible he could use as a weapon, or anything else. And the situation was way past one he could talk his way out of.

Sleeping with the Captain's wife had severely limited his options.

If they caught him, they were going to kill him, and it wouldn't be quick. He'd witnessed the hideously sadistic side of the Captain's temper when the Engineer had tried making excuses for one systems failure too many. He wasn't willing to suffer like that. A quick death, if that was what waited on the other side of the airlock, was preferable.

Neroy's dataLink accessed the ancient safety protocols and teased them aside. He entered the cramped airlock. The inner door slid shut behind him with a rusty groan. A stirring of air came from the ceiling vents, then a slow hiss from the opening outer door as the pressure seals released. Neroy was dimly aware of fists beating against the inner door's armoured window as he launched forward. Everything slowed down as the outer airlock rushed towards him. Then he was past it, and out of the ship.

He fell the short distance to the ground, landing hard in a spray of dust.

Neroy took in a blur of beaten, ochre earth, then he was staggering up and jogging towards a huddle of shabby buildings. A roaring tore up from the ship's engines, then a thermal wave slammed into him as he dived behind a rough wooden shed.

He jammed his hands over his ears to drown out the screaming thrusters, ground shaking as the ship rose off the ground. Neroy squinted up as the trader slowly hauled itself back into the sky, then rapidly gained speed until it was a shrinking dot amongst the clouds. He coughed, and swayed to his feet. Neroy felt a pain in his leg. He dug something hard out of his pocket that had gotten wedged-in. It sparkled dully when he held it up.

A golden chip, from the casino back on Earth.

A collection of primitive structures surrounded what looked to be a basic Landing Ring for smaller craft, although there weren't any ships there. The place was deserted.

Neroy slowly circuited the Ring, picking up a foul, earthy smell when he was halfway round. He followed it behind a building to find a huge pile of animal dung, and next to that a hand-painted sign: *Welcome to De'Spyr.* Neroy sighed. Evolving circumstances had necessitated an unscheduled transfer from the Proxima-bound ship he'd initially boarded from Earth. The traders he'd travelled with after that had mentioned their destination, but he'd become distracted during the voyage. He'd never heard of De'Spyr, but it was clearly deep in the back of beyond. That was the thing about rapid transfers through the wormhole network. All too easy to fall off the beaten path. He tried his dataLink. Nothing.

He noticed a faint hubbub. A crowd was approaching, still some way off, but their angry shouts were increasingly audible. The one thing Neroy had picked up about this place from the crew was that they'd been planning to pull a fast one on whoever they were trading with, then leave. Immediately. Which was why he'd been forced to make a break from his bolthole when some of the traders had returned to the ship, a few moments ago. But now he needed to move before he got tangled up in whatever scam they'd pulled.

A squelching sounded from behind. Neroy wheeled round, then relaxed. A young man with the worst skin problems he'd ever seen had appeared from a shed and was attacking the dung heap with a wooden spade, scooping some of the dripping brown slurry into a bucket. Barefoot, his rough woollen clothes were torn and ancient.

"Hey, kid," said Neroy. "Any idea where a man can get a ride into town?"

The boy cringed. He looked around, desperate to conjure up someone else who Neroy could plausibly be talking to. A shift in the wind brought the sounds of the mob a little nearer. They sounded angrier, now.

"Relax, kid," said Neroy, backing away. "I'm OK with walking, unless there's some alternative?"

After a final beseeching look at the dung hill, the boy faced Neroy, nervously fingering the wooden icon around his neck. "Uh…k-know that I do not, milord," he began, "but-"

A shout cut the boy off, as a stout, ruddy-faced man waddled swiftly around the dung heap from the other side. Dressed in the same medieval garb, he seemed a little further up the local food chain. "By the Saints! Apologies, milord! Hope I most sincerely that this peon has not yourself offended. Bozz!" He swiped the boy. "Remember your place, lad!"

Bozz was practically bending double as he bowed his head. "Pardon Sir, pardon!"

Neroy smiled. "No problem here, pal. But assuming you know where to find a taxi, could we get the hell out of here, please?" With a murderous glare at Bozz, the man beckoned obsequiously for Neroy to follow. A short way off he helped Neroy up into a cart pulled by a pair of Oxen analogues, hefty beasts with three sets of legs and a touch of lizardry in their ancestral DNA. From the smell of them, they were the generators of the dung. The continual stink was getting to Neroy, and he rested his head in his hands.

"Where to, milord?"

"No idea, pal," replied Neroy. "This dump was not on my itinerary." He strained, listening for the mob. But for the moment there was nothing. "Let's just head into town. Take me to the best joint you know. And let's try to avoid the welcome party."

The man cracked his whip. He gave Neroy a knowing wink as the beasts hauled the cart away, breaking off from the main road. A dip in the landscape revealed a distant city and, somewhat nearer, a forest, running up the slope of an enormous, smoking volcano. Something was moving through the woodland, the motion obvious even at this distance.

A titanic version of one of the Oxen analogues suddenly emerged from the treeline. The driver was clearly unperturbed, so Neroy put his feet up and concentrated on breathing through his mouth to avoid the smell from its smaller cousins. Plenty of opportunities to be had in feudal societies, even one as low-tech as this. Inequality meant a concentration of wealth in the hands of an unscrupulous elite, and in a place like this, such people tended to be especially vicious. That was OK. It just meant you had to figure out the rules a little more carefully before you started breaking them. So take it slow. Shit-shoveler to cart driver to innkeeper should be a safe enough social distance to travel in one day. And there was another bright side. He'd wanted a place where no one was looking for him.

On that basis, he couldn't have chosen anywhere better.

After a while the cart reached the city wall. They rode through a gate manned by armoured guards, who watched them disinterestedly. A creaking noise from above drew Neroy's attention. An iron gibbet swung slowly in the wind. Inside was a skeletal, mutilated figure. Neroy shuddered. Hopefully they were dead. Puddles dotted the broken streets, with things-that-looked-like-chickens-but-weren't pecking at rotting garbage.

Whenever the cart slowed, deformed beggars rushed out from the shabby wattle huts that tottered between more solid townhouses. The streets were quiet, but as they reached their destination, a line of slaves, each with a spiked iron collar linked by a single twisting chain, shuffled out of a sodden yard. They had all been recently blinded. "Welcome to Xaancholi, milord," said the driver, jumping down in a spray of what Neroy hoped was mud, "being the jewel in the sword of De'Spyr, and no mistake."

He stuck out his hand, palm-up. "May your day be blessed."

The Inn was perfect. Neroy ran out of people to play cards with after a few one-sided games, but that generated enough to pay for the best room they had, and a bottle plus a surprisingly decent cigar were proving to be good enough company now that card partners had dried up.

The place was well-equipped to meet the needs of offworlders, along with any locals who could afford it. Its stone walls were covered with unidentifiable animal skins, shields and a variety of bladed weapons clearly intended to be decorative, yet which still looked dangerously functional. With small windows, the tavern was full of dark corners. A hearty fire roared, its flickering glow complemented by a liberal spread of holoScreens.

Every nook had a smattering of religious knick-knacks, including fancier-looking versions of the square icon the boy had worn back at the landing circle. De'Spyr was enough of a backwater that it was still stuck deep in a spiritual phase. Not that that was a problem. People could believe whatever they wanted. At the end of the day, it was just another angle to exploit.

Neroy sauntered over to the bar for a beer. The bottle he'd been nursing was a local spirit whose name he couldn't pronounce, and it was quietly lethal.

"Little quiet today?" ventured Neroy as the landlady drew him a flagon of ale. A hefty, no-nonsense type, she gave the impression of running a tight ship.

"Not normally like this," she scowled, indicating a scattering of paunchy merchant types with lots of heavy jewellery. "Normally your lot can't wait to come down planetside from that there Orbital Hub. On account of it being so dull and lacking in diversion, or so I've heard. Make some money, have a drink or two. Everyone's happy, Saints willing."

She slammed Neroy's flagon down, spilling a good inch of beer onto the swampy bar-top. "Normally, that is," she spat, glaring at Neroy as though holding him personally responsible for her lack of custom.

"Sorry to hear that," Neroy said, sipping his beer. It was watery and rather stale. "Buy you a drink?" He slid a heavy gold De'Spyr Shylling across the counter.

"Hmph," she snorted, pouring herself a large glass of something expensive-looking. She downed it, then sat on a stool behind the bar, producing a creak of protest. "Be thanking you, I needed that." She sighed, then lowered her voice.

"You know what I've heard?"

Neroy leaned in. "I can't imagine."

"You'll laugh," she began. "Think me ignorant and all. But normally we get a good flow of trade from mining Systems. Our Royals are always wanting precious ores and whatnot. From Systems like Altraxia and, you know. Kumeiijm'a..."

Neroy gulped some ale to cover his surprise. That name again.

"Well, apparently there's been a couple of ships as have gone missing. Or leastways they haven't turned up here. And you know why?"

Neroy shook his head energetically, pantomiming intense interest.

She breathed the word in a quiet exhalation. "*Aliens.*"

Neroy took another gulp, this time to cover the sneer on his lips. He'd need another flagon soon. "Ah, really?"

"Oh yes, and it's not just my Inn, you know. Everyone in town's saying the same thing." She tapped the side of her nose. "And there's no rumour what flowers without a seed of truth. The authorities won't never admit it, of course, but some of us know what's really out there. Don't you go believing everything you hear from those what says they knows better—the galaxy's a big old place, if you hadn't of heard."

She sat back, running her finger around the rim of her empty glass. Neroy bought her another, and turned the conversation to information of a different kind. His dataLink implant was useless on De'Spyr, so he paid her to arrange the supply of a local communications device and a connection to the planet's primitive worldNet. He needed to put the word out, sooner rather than later. His card winnings might cover a second night at the Inn, but no more.

After some careful probing, the Innkeeper mentioned a local gang who might want an offworld specialist, but that wasn't for him. He never looked to work in a team at the best of times, and that went double for a place like this. The landlady's other suggestion was to watch out for a man named Constanz, who frequented the place. A procurer of women, he was apparently well-connected with the local elite, and easily recognised on account of his enormous size. But that was all she had to offer, and as the quiet afternoon turned into a drab evening, Neroy climbed the stairs to his room above the bar and fell into a deep, exhausted sleep.

Neroy woke screaming. He stared frantically around the darkened bedroom as the remains of his nightmare slunk away. He'd been on fire. Somewhere awful. The pain from the flames was still making him shake. And something else, something worse. Laughter? But he couldn't hold on to it. Mercifully, the memories were already fading. Neroy fumbled his clothes on and headed for the door. Despite the hour, muffled voices were coming from the bar.

It was the middle of the night, but the place was still half open. The doors and windows were shuttered tight, lights dimmed. A thin, afterhours crowd was scattered about the place, mostly locals in quiet corners.

None of them looked friendly.

Neroy sat at the bar under the brightest lights in the room. The barman casually placed something in front of him. A scarred rectangle of dark glass-like material. Neroy wasn't sure what it was, then icons stuttered to life around the edges. A faint signal connected to his dataLink. It was the device the landlady had promised. He nodded his thanks then accessed the worldNet, grateful for distraction from the lingering unease.

Neroy splashed local information on his dataLens, digital content overlaying a wall display of what looked like implements of torture, directly in his line of sight. Arranged over the hearth, Neroy had previously assumed they were fireplace tools, but now he wasn't so sure. The bladed edges were rather too medical-looking for cutting wood, and the flickering fire illuminated what seemed to be rusty patches of dried blood.

It made a suitably depressing backdrop for what he was rapidly learning about De'Spyr. The place was a feudal world, and primitive at that. A patchwork of independent city-states of which Xaancholi was the largest, it had been at a medieval technology level when EarthFed made contact two hundred years ago, and it hadn't advanced significantly since then, according to the most recent surveys. Deliberately, it seemed. The noble classes used imported tech sparingly to maintain their status. Its use was strictly controlled, and for the vast majority of the populace, life remained savage, precarious and grinding.

Most of the planet was rural. Jungle covered the major continents, teeming with ferocious megafauna like the enormous lizard-things he'd glimpsed. And a lot of them looked much less friendly than that. The noble class seemed pretty lethal too, with the local Royals, notionally rulers of the whole planet, coming across like the biggest shits in the toilet bowl, with a particular taste for feral internecine squabbling.

Neroy killed the data feed. The worldNet was basic and jury-rigged, with reams of fractured information he couldn't access properly. Might be useful contacts in there who needed to hire someone like him, but he wasn't going to find them tonight. He scanned the bar. The landlady had told him earlier there were only a couple of places like this in town. Very expensive for locals, and most of them weren't allowed in to mix with offworlders, even in theory.

Anyone in here had connections of some sort. If they looked like they ran with a bad crowd, they probably knew the kind of people he needed to meet.

A group of women dressed to tempt sat at a corner table, draped around a gaudily-dressed hulk of a man who smiled solicitously at Neroy as their eyes met. That must be Constanz, the pimp the innkeeper had mentioned. Neroy sent a bottle over with his compliments. The man shoved one of the girls to her feet. She tottered over, touched a manicured hand to the bar to steady herself, then stood there swaying. Her outfit was revealing but borderline tasteful, painted face subtly emphasising her features. Her makeup almost hid her black eye, but the swelling defeated efforts at concealment.

"He sent me over to get you," she slurred. Neroy smiled and started to reply, but she stumbled in close. "He's an animal. Hit me earlier. You believe that? Said I wasn't getting enough trade." She glared at her pimp. "Screw him. Wanna go somewhere else? There's a shaman, runs a wild place near the palace. We could go there instead." She stared at him unsteadily. "It's unbelievable there. Anything goes."

Neroy was tempted. On a world like De'Spyr the barriers blurred between current civilisation and what had come before. Whatever that was, on a planet like this. Such as shamans, for example. Dirt magicians. Witches. Whatever they called psychics here. In an ancient city like this, anything could be out there. The EarthFed surveys he'd just read looked like they'd barely scratched the surface. But no. Best to focus on immediate options. And a world like this was far too unpredictable. "Sounds wonderful, honey. Maybe another time."

"What's the matter, baby? Don't you trust me?"

He smiled. "Not even slightly. But don't take it personally. Just a general policy."

The pimp introduced himself as Constanz De'Majel IV. Neroy's bottle quickly emptied, and they were well into a second one before long. Constanz claimed to be minor nobility, an educated person forced into the harsh world of commerce by a chain of unfortunate events on which he declined to elaborate. A huge man, his robes strained to contain his muscled frame. He had an undertone of bitterness, despite his convivial efforts. If Neroy was going to probe him, it would be safer to take the edge off.

"If you don't mind me asking, Constanz—do you mind if I call you Constanz?"

The pimp rolled his shoulders in generous assent.

"I was wondering what an enlightened man like yourself was doing in this line of work? Surely you must have a wide range of business opportunities."

Constanz stared darkly into his glass. "This planet is an unforgiving place, Neroy. One mistake, and everyone turns their back on you."

"That's terrible," said Neroy, topping him up. "But surely there must be enterprises requiring specialists—men of intelligence and experience? Given the right opportunity?"

Constanz swatted his hand. "Naturally. In fact, I'm a specialist myself."

"In what area would that be?"

The big man smiled arrogantly. "Earthers. Your technology, and so-called culture." He gestured lazily at his girls. "It's what enables me to conduct my business effectively, in this and... other markets."

Neroy intimated that he had broad business interests. Constanz said there were a variety of options available, some illicit, involving members of the local elite as potential partners. Suddenly Neroy imagined him at the head of the angry mob who'd been so keen to meet the traders yesterday.

"Now," began Neroy, "local enterprises of a more... informal nature. Would their operations ever require specialist-"

"But that's all so shallow!" interrupted Constanz. "Who would fawn for the favour in business of one's so-called superiors, when pleasures of the mind and body are so much more appealing?" He fished a small leather book out of his pocket and flourished it, waiting for Neroy to ask about it.

"Of course," smiled Neroy, with an inner sigh. "I feel the same way. So what's the book?"

Constanz laid it down carefully. "An ancient chronicle of our planet's Holy Texts, which I... borrowed from the Royal library." He went on to expound on several millennia's worth of De'Spyr's history, reading some of his favourite extracts aloud. Neroy noticed one of the girls falling asleep, the bruised one he'd talked to earlier. The drink in her hand began to tip. He reached out for it but the glass suddenly flipped, flooding the table with ruby wine.

Constanz snatched up the book. He roared at the girl, then slapped her.

"Easy, Constanz," Neroy said. "The girl fell asleep. It was just-"

"She's ruined the book!" shouted the pimp, shaking the dripping tome. "Look at it! It's useless now—just like all you harlots!" He viciously clouted the girl next to him with it. She cowered, terrified.

Neroy moved his hand closer to a hefty candlestick. "OK, pal. Enough already. The girl did us a favour there, I was starting to nod off myself."

The pimp shook a meaty fist. "Speak of my planet's history with respect!" His eyes shone. "The royal history you dismiss is but a small part of our culture! Our traditions. And a recent part at that!" He adopted a zealot's stare.

"The Old Ways. Old Gods. We used to sacrifice people here, before the Earth ships came." Constanz pointed at some tattered skins on the wall. "You see those?" He lowered his voice. "They're not from animals, my friend."

Neroy peered closer. There was a pinkish tone to some of them, beneath the soot. "Whatever magic ceremony they were used in, they've seen better days, friend."

Constanz sneered. "Magic. Religion. Whatever you Earthers call it, it's real, Sphinx. Rumours tell of an ancient temple beneath Xaancholi. A temple I shall see one day. A place of ancient wonders. Our wonders. That shall rise again!" He emptied his glass and tossed it away.

Neroy ordered another two bottles, which the pimp gracelessly accepted. Neroy filled their glasses, but kept his hand near the candlestick. "Ah, c'mon, Constanz. I mean, sure, there's a lot of strange stuff out there. I've been around. But we're both businessmen, right?

Constanz slammed his drink down. "We're nothing alike! You Earthers are utterly ignorant of the deep past's holy truths!"

Neroy raised an eyebrow. "Such as?"

The pimp seized up the sodden book. "Such as! The true nature of the forces behind the War in Heaven! That mystic cataclysm, millennia ago, that swept aside the civilisation of the ancients and sundered the worlds of men from one another. Until you cursed Earthers stumbled across the wormholes once more, and darkened our skies!"

"Ah, c'mon, Constanz. There's nothing supernatural about all that ancient history. Even I picked the basics up at school, and that's saying something."

Neroy lit a smoke. "Way back in everyone's pre-history, there was some earlier civilisation running everything. They had a war that screwed the wormholes up so badly, they only healed a few hundred years ago. Interstellar society collapsed and all the worlds were isolated for thousands of years. Yadda yadda yadda. Time passes, Earth gets back on its feet, re-discovers the wormhole system and sets up EarthFed. Until that fell apart ten years ago, everything went to shit again and here we all are."

He threw his butt in the fireplace. "The end."

"It's all about your precious technology, isn't it?" Constanz retorted. "But you're blind to the true nature of the reality lying behind your ships and your weapons."

"Sadly I don't have a ship, or money to buy passage. And the only weapon I have right now," said Neroy, tapping his temple, "is in here."

The pimp plunged on. "Take those wormholes you mentioned. Your scientists' theories can't fully account for them. Not really. Ask them! And the Gateway portals that activate them—you just patched up the decaying amplifier rings that were still there, back when you stumbled across the first one in your home System. You don't really know how they work, and you barely managed to fix them!"

"Maybe you'd just have preferred it to be De'Spyr that got there first. What would you have called your galactic empire, though, Constanz? De'SFed? Doesn't exactly roll off the tongue..."

Neroy poured them both a large one and settled back. The pimp hadn't hit him, and didn't look like he was about to. Not really. Despite his anger, he craved an audience. Neroy let him carry on. Crazy stuff about how the early wormhole trips had gone badly wrong until they partly figured the tech out, crews disappearing, leaving nothing but scorch marks inside the ships.

Constanz calmed a little, complaining how it was just an historical accident that Earth happened to be on an upwards technology curve when the wormholes healed. That it could just as easily have been Altraxia, or Magellus. As he talked it became clear that, despite his initial mystical rantings, technology was his passion, filtered through the resentful perspective of a younger brother aggrieved from not sitting at the grownup's table.

Which gave Neroy an idea.

He'd drunk enough that it was now a matter of staying focused, rather than drowning his night-time fears. Which made it time to wrap things up.

"Sorry Constanz," Neroy interrupted, "but that argument only goes so far. I mean, some worlds have that... killer instinct. Others don't. Whatever the tech level. Look what happened when EarthFed fell apart. Not to sound like a text book but, you know, the inter-System institutions all crumbled as you local Systems hived off. Military assets started getting grabbed by System Governments, and the Fleet pulled back to the Sol System."

"Exactly! That happened here," Constanz sneered. "Your navy ships fled like whipped puppies!"

"Yeah, but you guys must have been half asleep, you didn't grab shit after they left. Your Orbital station was run by an EarthFed Directorate, but you were so slow asserting jurisdiction, it went independent. No one planetside has any authority over it. So offworld travel's real limited. I mean, you ever been to the Orbital?"

Constanz deflated. "I have not had that pleasure."

Neroy leaned in. "It's quite something, even when you're used to it. An artificial world, floating there in space."

"I can imagine," sighed Constanz.

Neroy produced his worldNet device. "Like to see one?"

"What do you mean?"

"My dataLink implant can't integrate with much of anything on this planet.

"What would you have called your galactic empire, Constanz?"

But its storage and playback functions work fine, and I can shunt content to this thing. Care for a tour of Earth's Orbital? I still have the sensory brochure from when I was there a little while back..."

Constanz swiftly produced a battered headset which he connected to Neroy's device. Initially suspicious, his jaw slackened as he drank in Neroy's feed. It began with the Orbital tour brochure, aimed at pleasure travellers, showcasing the marvels of what had been EarthFed's most advanced Orbital facility.

Then Neroy switched to another set of files, the plans for the Dubblz job. Constanz was mesmerised by the portal generator and the droid suits and, as Neroy talked him through the intricacies of the job he'd planned and executed, the conversation's tone shifted to two enthusiasts discussing a topic of mutual fascination. Neroy made it clear he was looking to apply his skills locally, should any suitable opportunities exist.

When it was over Constanz laid the headset gently on the table.

"My apologies, Neroy. I fear I misjudged you. You're clearly a man of many talents—and no enthusiast for the Earth authorities, either. As it happens, I believe a Palace contact may well have urgent need for a man such as yourself."

Neroy smiled. "I'd appreciate it, Constanz. Be happy to pay a commission, too."

Constanz waved the offer away. "No need for anything so crude. I would benefit in other ways from such an introduction. Because you couldn't have known, but Xaancholi's Royal Family is... about to undergo a transition." He clapped Neroy painfully on the shoulder. "And in times of change, the value of the right man is far beyond measure."

Neroy just made it to the sink before he threw up a bellyful of alcohol. He drank slowly from the tap, then washed everything away. Neroy wasn't sure when he'd gotten to bed, but it had still been dark. It wasn't now, and the daylight streaming through the curtains made him wince. He hadn't dreamed again, or if he had he didn't remember.

But then, to his horror, thinking about his dreams summoned back the terror he'd suffered in the middle of the night, before he'd met Constanz. The shadows of the room retreated, the morning sun's heat becoming a familiar, scouring fire that seared his skin. Laughter echoed up out of nowhere, and he knew he wasn't alone. Then fear twisted into nausea, and he vomited again. This time he felt purged, and when he fell back into bed he was drained but clear-headed. The terror was gone, and the nightmare with it, slithered back inside the gap in his memories. The Cold Black Glass.

Neroy surveyed the Glass cautiously as he dressed, probing its edges without attempting to breach its frontiers, nervous of provoking another bout of nausea, or a worsened headache. The Gap's parameters felt well-established now. It started when he was in the middle of a job. A plush corporate hotel back in TC where he was working a long con. He'd been in his room, dressing for dinner. Then the curtain came down. When it rose again, five years had passed. He was on Kumeiijm'a. Dim recollections of a hospital, then sharper memories of a bar, planning a job with her. The woman in black. The woman who'd ended up knocking him on his ass and walking away, after which he'd sunk into a blurry torpor in Peach Heights, back on Earth.

So. Half a decade. The gap might not have started on a significant date, but it sure did end on one. Coincidence or not, the return of his hazy memories coincided exactly with the Fall of EarthFed. He smiled, a phrase from his worldNet research the night before coming to mind: *Two hundred and fifty years of co-created peace and prosperity, falling apart like a House of Cards.*

He'd always been good at using cards to create prosperity. Time to head to the Palace and see what hand he was going to be dealt.

The Palace of Xaancholi looked like it could be an extraordinary construction, Neroy thought. But to see it properly he'd have to get past the gibbets first. An obscuring screen of moaning, beseeching figures trapped within human-shaped metal cages stretched across the far end of Palace Square.

Neroy exited his carriage in the Square's centre, then loitered, unsure of decorum, before spotting a functionary in Royal livery weaving through the crowd. The man dodged across the busy Square, then strode between two cages in the middle of the row, the occupants of which appeared mercifully-deceased. Gaze fixed straight ahead, Neroy followed after. He flinched as one of the dead people's arms brushed his coat as he passed. Neroy couldn't stop himself from looking down. It was a child's hand, with small delicate fingers.

The Square continued on the other side of the gibbets, empty aside from a few Palace staff darting between official buildings. The cobbles terminated at the edge of parkland that rolled away until it lapped at the sides of the distant Palace. Neroy strode to the end of the Square and ducked behind a hedge. He sat on a wooden bench, taking a moment to focus on what loomed ahead, rather than what lay hanging behind him.

The Palace was vast, a redoubt of titanic proportions constructed by generations of Royals, each determined to outdo the previous occupants in an architectural arms race that had produced a sumptuous monstrosity. The flags, towers, battlements, and ramparts were endless, shameless, and thoroughly overwhelming. Neroy resolved to ignore the details as best he could as he began trudging forward.

Constanz had instructed Neroy to present himself at a side-entrance on the Eastern Wing near the kitchens, and announce who had sent him. The smell of roasted meat grew strong as Neroy made his way through the gardens, stomach emptier with every step. Breakfast had been a smoke in the carriage, so he plucked an apple as he passed a small orchard. The fruit had a zesty tang, and did a fine job of banishing the taste of the night before by the time he reached the kitchens.

The door was answered by a man in the same livery as the servant Neroy had followed across the Square. He led Neroy to a small reception room. After a while, a dignified-looking older man with a sharp black beard and flowing robes appeared, followed by a small retinue keeping a respectful distance. He inspected Neroy carefully.

"Welcome, Mr Sphinx," he said, arms held lightly behind his back. "I am Grand Vizier De'Majel. My cousin has spoken well of you, as a man whose rather specific skills may be just what is required... at this particular juncture in Royal society."

"Sounds intriguing, Grand Vizier. I-"

"No need to be so formal," smiled the Grand Vizier, raising an exquisitely-jewelled hand. "*Your Worship* shall suffice."

"Of course," nodded Neroy. "Might I ask-"

"You may not," replied the Grand Vizier. "It is a delicate matter, to be discussed privately. Come," he concluded, striding out of the room. Neroy jogged after, dodging around the slowly-moving knot of attendants.

"Nice place you got here, Your Worship," said Neroy. The corridor was a crude stone passageway with a rough floor. Centuries' worth of dripping water had scoured dark rivulets into the walls. The place reeked of damp, wood-smoke, and boiled vegetables.

The Grand Vizier smiled tolerantly at Neroy. "Do not waste time on flattery. I am not the one you need to impress. My disgraced cousin's summary of your... resumé was all that I required."

"He mentioned the bank job, I assume?"

"Indeed. Nothing like that is required here, of course. But I imagine your assignments vary greatly, according to circumstance and opportunity?"

Neroy nodded. The Vizier was clearly a sharp cookie. Which would make whatever this involved that little bit harder. "They do indeed, Your Worship. In fact—"

"But nevertheless, your core abilities would be applied in each new situation, yes? Situational judgement. Creative thinking. An amoral application of intuition, insight and logic." The Vizier raised a delicately-plucked eyebrow, sharpness in his eyes. "Rather like my own capabilities. With each change in Royal leadership I am required to support new agendas, accommodate new personalities and enact new priorities. As though nothing had ever changed."

"So how does-"

"A moment please." They had reached a large wooden door, flanked by two guards. The men were huge, wearing furs and chainmail with a blaster on one hip and a scimitar on the other. Each held a long spear that rested on the ground, their weapons angled-in towards each other, spear tips meeting in the middle of the doorway.

The Vizier spoke to them and they stood aside, opening the door to the Palace proper. Neroy and the Vizier walked through a succession of empty, echoing halls and banquet rooms, stuffed with a gaudy jumble of gilt statuary, painted urns, heavy wooden furniture, suits of armour and endless displays of ornate weaponry hanging over an equally endless number of huge stone fireplaces.

"Gets pretty cold in the winters, huh? What with all these-"

"Probably," replied the Vizier. "I wouldn't know. We always retire to the Southern Palace when the leaves begin to fall."

Neroy indicated a particularly ugly cluster of drab tapestries and dull, unpolished goblets on an antique sideboard that didn't look like it had been cleaned since it was made. "It's all very impressive, Your Worship. Haven't seen anything like this since the last time I was on Cassiopia. In fact-"

"Oh, indeed. De'Spyr is a rich world. We didn't suffer nearly so much as other planets, during the numberless aeons of The Isolation."

Neroy nodded politely. "Oh, indeed, Your Worship. I'm sure many of you didn't suffer at all."

The Vizier bristled. "You may view our system of government as archaic. Primitive, perhaps. But following the Fall of EarthFed, we endure as before. Stability is one of the many benefits monarchy brings. Earth is powerful, even now. But culturally? You are barbarians, sir. Without true care for your populace. Now, my debauched cousin is not the only student of your peoples' ways, Mr Sphinx. In fact, I inspired his interest. But even a fool could see that EarthFed, with its 'Functional Directorate' and 'Central Committee' was nothing but a corrupt, inefficient system, creaking at the seams, held together by—how do you put it—'robbing Peter to pay Paul'? Until the whole thing fell apart! And now? What remains of your government is a paranoid, dictatorial mess."

The Vizier paused, relishing the prospect of an offended rebuttal.

Neroy shrugged. "Sounds about right to me, Your Worship. Although it seems you know more about Earth's government than I do. Tell you the truth, as long as I can stay out of the government's way, I'm happy to let them get on with it. They work their patch, I work mine."

The Vizier sniffed disdainfully, then swept forward. They carried on until they reached the dingy corner of an especially dirty room. The Vizier produced a small key, and Neroy noticed the outline of a door set into the wall panels. With a quiet *click* the Vizier opened it. They walked through into a much smaller, but very ornate, chamber.

There was no one there. The Vizier instructed Neroy to wait, directing him to a couch under the room's only window, a vast pane of armoured glass. The window overlooked the gardens. The lawns stretched away from the palace until they reached a distant spread of forest. Beyond the faraway trees a faint haze of smoke rose from an enormous mountain. The volcano, he realised. Near the Landing Ring.

Neroy waited a moment, then slipped out the worldNet device. He'd messaged the Innkeeper from the carriage. Reading her reply, his pulse quickened. An offworld trade crew was scheduled to arrive at the Inn, with their ship landing at noon tomorrow.

That was very good news indeed. The Vizier seemed lethally smart, the last thing Neroy wanted in a potential client. He needed a way offworld, as soon as possible. If he hung around to the end of this job, whatever it was, it would likely be the end of him. But traders would expect a guy to pay his way with real currency—Earth credWafers, not the local beads of coloured glass he'd won gambling back at the Inn. EarthFed wasn't there to back up credWafers anymore. They'd become an unmanaged interstellar currency that no one ultimately owned, but which nevertheless creaked along, held together by the mutual self-interest of everyone who needed to use them.

And if he wanted to get offplanet tomorrow, he was going to need plenty of them.

Neroy turned his thoughts to the imminent meeting. The Vizier was the one he had to watch, but he wasn't the actual client. Truth was, he didn't know who the Big Cheese was on the other side of the door. According to the worldNet, Xaancholi was currently ruled by Emperor Abibadazzad VIII. But he hadn't made public appearances for some time, and Neroy hadn't been able to get anything solid out of the online data slurry in terms of the line of succession, dominant candidates within it, or mechanisms thereof.

Constanz had mentioned a time of transition, and the Vizier himself had emphasised the need to accommodate new rulers in the ongoing execution of his duties. Perhaps change was coming to a head on De'Spyr.

The soft ticking of a clock drew Neroy's attention. An enormous, gilded mechanism rested on a table across the room from him, its glass cover showcasing an intricate cogwheeled interior. Neroy tracked the spinning clockwork, the mechanism of action drawing his gaze in towards the centre of the device where the masterwheel slowly turned. As his gaze settled on the timepiece's core, he started in his seat. An eyeless skull was staring back at him. The chronometer had been built around a mummified human head, frozen in a scream of agonised despair, above whose forehead the central wheel was set.

"Shall we go in, Mr Sphinx?" asked the Vizier. He had slipped silently back into the room and was standing in the far corner, beckoning through a doorway. "Princess Alloria awaits."

The throne room was an ancient place. The windows were slits, set high-up. Darkness pressed in from all sides, held feebly at bay by flaming torches. The room was almost bare aside from a crude throne on a marble dais, seat softened by a scattering of straw. But the throne was currently unoccupied.

"Princess Alloria will be with us presently," whispered the Grand Vizier. "She believes in making a proper entrance, you see. Effect is most important to her. This room, for example. And her currently favoured attire. It's all modelled on classic historical periods. Distilling the best of antiquity for use in the present, one might say." The Vizier nodded in agreement with himself, and said no more. He and Neroy stood in silence, waiting.

A side-door opened and Princess Alloria swept in, her presence filling the room. A statuesque, voluptuous woman, her striking beauty conveyed a fierce arrogance. Clothed in strips of fur with thigh-length boots made from some rough, dark pelt, she had a savage look, like some hunter from deep pre-history. A mane of wild black hair cascaded down her back past her waist, bunched at the top of her head behind a jewelled, wireframe tiara.

Two enormous guards followed her as she catwalked to the throne. She draped herself over it, one leg lolling over the side. The way she carried herself made it clear she believed she was totally irresistible. That any man—even an offworlder—would do anything she wanted. Who knew, Neroy thought. Maybe she was right.

The Vizier bowed deeply. "And now, Mr Sphinx, may I humbly present Her

Exalted Imperial Majesty, Princess Alloria."

The Princess affected to notice Neroy for the first time, inspecting him with distaste. "We do not receive many visitors on De'Spyr these days, Mr Sphinx," she drawled in a bored tone. "An unexpected stopover?"

"Not at all, Princess," Neroy replied. "De'Spyr is justly famous—I've always wanted to see it."

She rose and slowly descended the dais steps, approaching Neroy with an imperious gait. The Princess stopped a short distance from him, appraising him coldly. Neroy knew this was the crucial moment. Her entrance was intended to make a specific impression, to generate a reaction she was now looking out for. A tell that he'd been hooked, that she could bend him to her will. He let his eyes wander over her body, doing his best to make it look like he was failing to keep himself in check. To make it more obvious, he flicked his tongue across his lips as quickly as he could.

Princess Alloria sneered, and gracefully extended a hand. She wore a single ring inset with a blood-red jewel. Neroy bent to kiss it. The stone was cold. Despite its polished appearance, it felt rough against his lips.

The Princess placed her hands on her hips. She angled her chin in his direction. "Please. You did not plan on visiting us at all. You were ejected from your ship, after the Captain caught you with his wife."

Neroy gave a small bow. "You're very well-informed, Majesty. How may I serve?"

The Princess walked back towards the door she'd entered by. The guards made to follow her, but she signalled them to stay. Once the three of them were inside the anteroom, the Vizier closed the door behind them. It had a secluded, study-like feel. Bookcases lined the room, stuffed with ancient leather tomes and sheaves of rolled-up parchment scrolls. A merry fire burned in the grate. But whatever was over the fireplace was concealed by a set of recently-installed drapes.

The gentle scuff of a shoe told Neroy someone was behind him.

A bald, cadaverous man in austere black clothes was standing in the corner of the room, next to the door. Neroy felt a confusing pressure in his head. He should have noticed the man as he'd entered the room. Must have walked right past him. But Neroy hadn't registered him at all. The pressure in his head suddenly diffused, clouding his senses and making his thoughts feel transparent, as though something had unlocked his mind, like a book being opened. Then the sharpness of the room came rushing back. The man in black bowed to the Princess and departed.

The Vizier smiled. "Just a simple psychic scan to ensure you are who we think you are, Mr Sphinx. The Princess has many enemies. I'm sure you understand."

Neroy fought the temptation to shake his head like a wet dog. "Of course. Did I pass the audition?"

"Indeed," replied the Vizier. "If you hadn't, we wouldn't be conversing so delightfully. But now, we may proceed."

Princess Alloria was gazing into the fire. She spun on her heel, and addressed him without preamble. "I hear you are an exceptional thief."

Neroy thought it was probably safe to stop bowing, but even so he gave her a polite nod. "That's true Ma'am—what do you want me to steal?"

"I don't want you to steal anything, Mr Sphinx. I wish you to return something to its rightful owner—discreetly."

"Hmm."

"*Hmm*, Mr Sphinx?"

"Just, ah, sounding a note of professional caution, Princess. Putting something back—that can often be a little more… *challenging*, Majesty. What is it?"

Princess Alloria walked to the fireplace and tapped one of the hearth stones. It swung open, revealing a concealed hiding place. The Princess drew out a long, tubular bag made from patches of light-coloured leather, crudely stitched together. It looked brand new. She glided back towards Neroy, but stopped out of reach. He stepped forward, but she held up her hand. "Keep your distance! This is not for the hands of offworlders!"

She opened the bag and drew the object out. It was a crude wooden staff, covered with runic inscriptions, a rough gemstone inset in one end. Holding it in both hands, she offered it to Neroy for inspection. Her grip on it was vice-like.

"Behold! The Staff of Zathros!" breathed the Princess. "Whosoever wields it shall have the throne on this world!"

There was a hush in the room. Neroy was plainly expected to respond, but he didn't have enough information to know what the angle should be. So the least-risky option was honesty. In situations like these, playing stupid was a great way to end up playing dead. Without the playing part.

Neroy swallowed hard. "Last I heard, De'Spyr had an Emperor. Well, at least Xaancholi does. You're a little too… womanly for that to be you. Your Majesty."

The Princess turned towards the fireplace. "Indeed. My uncle rules at present, as the staff is held by him."

"Doesn't look that way to me..."

"The succession is governed by strict rules. Seizing the Staff is not enough—power may only be transferred within the Royal Family during certain phases of the moons."

"And if it's not that time of the month…"

The Princess was suddenly furious, glaring at the bag. "Then the holder can claim nothing—and will be put to death. Only commoners may seize the Staff at any time."

"So why do-"

"My consort was not one for such subtleties." The Princess reached for the cord with which the drapes were parted, an anticipatory smile playing on her lips. Neroy glanced at the Vizier, but he was standing impassively by the door.

"I see," Neroy said. "So you need me to return the Staff unnoticed, presumably with a mind on future withdrawal, at a more auspicious time. However, I assume there's some element of challenge involved, or you'd have done it yourself. Where is it normally kept?"

The Princess yanked the cord. The drapes swung open, revealing a huge artwork drawn on an enormous piece of cracked, ancient leather.

The details were overwhelming. An insanely dense layering of scratchy hand-drawn curves twisted round each other, forming an intricate, nested swirl of lines that curled and unfolded in a manner whose complexity denied the eye any immediate sense of overall pattern, or meaning. Neroy blinked, looked away, then returned to it. And then he realised what it was. It was a map.

A map of a maze.

The Princess had been savouring Neroy's confusion, but she saw he had grasped its meaning. "Behold!" she announced with relish. "The Labyrinth of Xarr!"

"...great."

Now he knew what it was, Neroy's mind started getting into gear. Semi-consciously he fumbled for a smoke, the Princess shrugging her permission for him to light up when he caught himself and raised a questioning eyebrow in her direction.

He returned to the details of the map as the smoke slowly filled his lungs. The maze was fiendishly complicated, with what he could now see were pictograms at different points indicating what looked like soldiers, pits, lava, spiders, snakes, spikes and underground rivers, although there were many icons whose meaning he couldn't begin to guess at, and the ones he tentatively identified could well have been something else. Neroy's absorption was such that he didn't realise the Princess was speaking again until she'd clearly been doing so for a little while.

"...the Staff is usually kept in a chamber at the very centre of the maze," she was saying, "under this Palace. Protecting it are traps and guardians beyond measure, maintained in secrecy by the Brotherhood of Xarr!"

Neroy felt it wise to clarify that he had, in fact, been paying close attention all along. He stepped closer to the Princess, observing what he hoped was the necessary respectful distance. "Yet your consort breached it successfully—and returned. Why can't we just get him to do it again?"

The Princess shook her head. "That won't be possible."

"Why not?"

Princess Alloria held up the tubular staff-bag.

"What do you think I used to make this?"

Refreshments had been brought and consumed. Whatever they drank at the Palace, it was a hell of a lot smoother than the local hooch Neroy had endured back at the Inn. Savouring the last drops of whatever-it-was-they'd-just-poured-for-him, Neroy cast an appreciative eye over the Princess as she leaned across a table, scrutinising documents with the Vizier. Trying to tame that one would probably get a man killed. Then again, it would probably be worth it.

The Princess muttered something to the Vizier. They put the documents away, returning their attentions to Neroy. They talked him through the details of the Labyrinth, starting at the outer edge and working inwards along the sole winding true path through the maze, expanding on each lethal trap and obstacle.

For each problem, Neroy could see a solution. At least on an individual basis. A jet pack would get him over the pits, and poison gas was easy to circumvent with a breatherMask. But it was turning into quite a shopping list and they weren't even halfway there. With an effort he tried to focus on the map, apparently stolen from the Brotherhood by the unfortunate consort. But as they talked, Neroy's attention kept straying to the bag, which Princess Alloria still had draped over her shoulder. Eventually, she noticed.

"You seem drawn to this, Mr Sphinx," she said, holding it up.

Neroy sighed. "It's just... we're facing a considerable challenge here, Your Majesty. Couldn't you just have asked your consort how he did it—*before* you turned him into a piece of luggage?"

The Princess' stare narrowed. "My Royal anger was aroused."

Neroy paused to light up again. "I'll have to keep that in mind."

They continued reviewing the map, spiralling in towards the centre, until their survey reached the end of the deadly path and they arrived at the vast central chamber.

Neroy pointed to the demonic ideogram within. "Can you tell me what this symbol means? It's not like any of the others."

"The one at the centre? Indeed. It is the final, ultimate defence—the monstrous Raknak!"

Neroy peered closer. It had been hard to make out before, but now he knew it was some kind of creature, the lines resolved into an unlikely cross between a lobster and a dinosaur. Whatever it was, judging by the scale, it was enormous. Which presented the beginnings of an idea. One plausible enough to convince them both that Neroy was someone they could rely on, at least until he had everything in place, and was ready to move. "This Raknak. What does it eat?"

"Naught but flesh! And it must devour its own weight every day, else-"

"Then that's our *in*, your Majesty," Neroy said, excitedly. The Princess' eyes flared at the interruption. But she let him continue.

"Whoever runs this labyrinth's got to be feeding it a mountain of meat every day. We figure out where it's coming from, smuggle me in with it… and I'll take it from there. Getting out past the traps should be a lot easier than getting in—the whole thing's intended to prevent easy inward travel."

As Neroy spoke, a cunning expression spread over the Princess' face. She drew closer than she had before.

"I see your capacity for guileful scheming is well-developed." She smiled slowly. "How exciting."

He could feel her breath on his face, sweet and hot and musky. He felt acutely aware of her body, a sudden tautness in his chest. She really was magnificent. The Raknak angle gave him the basis for further planning, and the shopping list was writing itself. The Princess offered a tempting bonus, but that was probably a great way to get your fingers burned, along with the rest of you, after she tied you to a stake and tossed on a match once she'd gotten what she wanted. But depending what she did to you before that, it could be a risk worth taking.

The Vizier clearly thought so too. Stationed by the door, his eyes were boring holes into Neroy over the Princess' shoulder. Anyone who entered the Labyrinth might be well-advised to bring the Vizier along, in case the Raknak hadn't gotten enough to eat. That should make subsequent negotiations with the Princess a little less treacherous.

Neroy nodded respectfully and took a step back. "Yes indeed, Your Majesty. In one way, the excitement of my work is its own reward. But in another, regrettably more commercial way..."

The Princess shrugged her lightly muscled shoulders. "Your price?"

"A million credWafers. Half up front, half on completion. Plus expenses for a few specialist items I'll need to get the job done. Assuming someone can help me procure the offworld tech I need?"

The Princess agreed disdainfully to Neroy's terms as though detailed discussion, let alone negotiation, was entirely beneath her. Assigning the Vizier to help Neroy with the sourcing of supplies, her tone became severe.

"Time is the crucial factor here, Mr Sphinx. Should the theft of the Staff be discovered, all would be lost. And as a fellow conspirator, your punishment would be equal to mine. I presume I need not describe it in order for you to accept that it would be hideous, drawn-out and utterly humiliating."

"Indeed, Majesty," said Neroy. "Shall we meet tomorrow morning, to confirm the final details?"

The Princess grinned dangerously. "That shall suffice, Mr Sphinx."

Neroy's heart pounded as he forced a smile, then bowed. "Until tomorrow, Majesty."

Neroy surveyed the chaos of Xaancholi's tumbledown harbour front with half an eye as the Vizier's carriage slowly approached the Grand Bazaar. Endless piers and jetties spidered-out over the waters of the Great Inland Ocean, drawing in a constant stream of goods from across De'Spyr, borne by an armada of steamships, sailboats, ocean liners and smaller yachts that darted in and about.

On the port's fringes, an armoured fishing vessel was being pulled by an enormous, harnessed sea serpent towards a processing plant, a mile-long trail of bloody fish innards in its wake. The place stank of sewage, saltwater and smoke from ships' engines, the rough caws of enormous, mangy seabirds mixing with the broken cries of the stevedores who swarmed the piers, hauling everything ashore.

Set back from the shoreline was the Grand Bazaar itself, a vast dome formed from a lattice of bronze girders containing city-block sized panes of crystal glass. The ocean-green crystal made it look as though sprays of seawater had frozen in place, remaining permanently onshore to enclose a captive patch of dry land.

The carriage was approaching the main entrance, an expansive gateway leading into the heart of the Bazaar. But they didn't stop. Instead, the carriage continued around the Bazaar's perimeter, then broke off, threading its way through a series of dilapidated stone warehouses until they reached a semi-derelict building at the very edge of the Bazaar district. The place was discreetly but heavily guarded.

Once they were inside, its hollowed-out interior was revealed to contain a pressureDome, the kind of temporary smartFabric construction usually found on early-stage Colony worlds. Just inside its airlock sat a spindly, nervous Altraxian trader, he and his wares safely hidden away from De'Spyr's regular citizenry. The place was packed with the very best the interstellar economy had to offer.

Backed by the Princess' credit line, Neroy lost himself in the tools of his trade. Before long he had built up a small, expensive pile that should signal he was taking the whole endeavour very seriously indeed. He made a show of appraising it all carefully, picking everything up and assessing it with an expert's eye.

As he did, he adjusted the plan-within-a-plan he'd come up with to mesh with the materials he'd assembled, all selected to meet the expectations of anyone who'd been paying attention to what he'd said he was planning to do. Such as the Grand Vizier. Throughout, the man had hovered at a distance, observing everything, missing nothing. Now it felt to Neroy like it was time to justify his approach, and create enough space to move on to the next stage.

Neroy picked up a small black disc and tossed it to the Vizier, who caught it nervously, almost dropping it.

"Stun gas grenade," explained Neroy. "More appropriate for live obstacles than anything explosive, when you're working in a closed environment of uncertain structural stability. Don't worry, Your Worship," said Neroy, plucking the grenade from the Vizier's hand. "The safety's on." He moved on to finger a neatly-folded white cloth on the checkout table. It was hard to focus on properly, even when he looked straight at it. Your eyes slid right off.

"And this beauty? You can't beat a decent chamCloak. Slip this baby on and you'll merge right into the scenery. Any trouble you can't fight your way through, you can just slip right around it." Truth to tell, he hadn't expected to find Exotic Tech like the chamCloak here, reverse-engineered by EarthFed's Military-Industrial complex from some ancient artefact. He'd heard of such devices but never seen one before, although the control interface seemed clear. Neroy hadn't asked the dealer where he'd obtained it, but the trader had obviously felt the need to dispose of it somewhere way off the beaten track. Like De'Spyr.

"And a jet pack," continued Neroy, indicating a plaSteel backpack on the table, small nozzles protruding from the bottom. "I guess you might be wondering-"

"Yes, yes," dismissed the Vizier. "I'm sure this would all be fascinating to a fellow practitioner of your sordid trade, but I've heard enough." He snapped his fingers at the trader, lurking nearby. "You! Have these items delivered to

Princess Alloria, immediately."

"Everything, sire?" asked the trader, greed on his face. "Some of these items are most expensive, and-"

"Deliver it all, I say!" ordered the Vizier. "The grenades, the cloak, the flying device—all of it! Including..." He trailed off, attention caught by a baroque bronze mask, attached by a coiling tube to a small tank. The Vizier scowled at it. "This—what is this?"

"breatherMask," said Neroy. "So I can be submerged in Raknak meat, then get smuggled in and still be alive and kicking when I come out the other side. Which reminds me. You and I need to discuss how we find out where that stuff comes from. When-"

"Cease your prattling!" snapped the Vizier. "It is... a sensitive matter. We shall discuss it later."

"...OK," said Neroy. "No problem." Whatever the Vizier's angle was here, it would have to wait. "But look," he said, gesturing towards the airlock in what he assumed was the Bazaar's general direction. "There's a few more items I need to pick up that this guy doesn't have." Items the Vizier didn't need to know about. "So what say you drop me off at the Bazaar for a couple of hours?"

"Very well," replied the Vizier, smiling dangerously. "But I shall accompany you myself. You are a guest here, Mr Sphinx. As an honourable host, I seek to smooth your passage in every way."

It hadn't taken Neroy long to give the Vizier the slip. Adept as the man might have been at navigating Palace politics, Neroy awarded him precisely zero out of ten for keeping track of an evasive quarry in a crowded environment. The Bazaar's interior was vast and dimly lit, the dark glass of the dome rising far overhead. Almost invisible in the gloom, the crystal ceiling's cyan tint produced a sea-green murk at ground level, accompanied by an undersea chill.

The layout was chaotic, a warren of stalls arranged around broad avenues from which meandering side alleys split off randomly. The canvas stalls ranged from small refreshment pens to huge tents packed with anything imaginable that could be crammed into a box, packet, case or bottle, hung from a rack or displayed on a counter. A damp, spicy smell hung in the air with strands of white vapour drifting along each thoroughfare, expelled from the outlet grates of the underground steam system powering the place.

The small tavern Neroy was sitting outside was near the middle of the Bazaar, next to a hardware tent where he'd picked up a pair of glass cutters, along with a few other sundries. He'd meant to stop at one drink, but then two had become three, and now he was in no particular hurry to find the Vizier. There had to be some kind of surveillance system in a place like this, and he was sitting under a street light in the middle of a main avenue. So let the man come to him.

Neroy pushed away his glass. All of a sudden, he wasn't feeling too hot. Then something inside him *twisted*, and he felt a blackness rising. Neroy thought he was about to vomit, but he gripped the table hard. After a moment it passed.

There was a kid sat begging across from the bar, some skinny little girl holding out a chipped wooden bowl. Empty, as far as he could tell. He walked over. She looked up at him, a small spark of hope in her eyes. It had been a long, long time, but he still remembered what that had felt like. Neroy smiled and emptied his pockets into the bowl until it began to overflow. The kid watched the coins spill over the sides, disbelieving. She jumped up and ran. He watched her skitter down the avenue, and duck into a side alley.

After that he just wandered around for a while.

The smell of flesh and blood snapped him out of it. Looking around, he saw he'd meandered into the meat section of the market. The Vizier still hadn't caught up with him, so what the hell. Might as well look into the Raknak angle. He walked around a little, and greased a few palms. The word on the street, such as it was, led him to a mid-sized pavilion set back from the main drag, partway down a dingy alley. Neroy was no specialist, but the stock was sparse and lousy-looking. Not a winning combination. The place was heavy on six-eyed flies, but very low on customers. Prosperous-looking though, so something was clearly off, in addition to just the merchandise.

The only guy working in the place had an evil look to him, but Neroy sauntered in. He was an offworlder, and working for the Princess. What the hell were these people going to do to him?

"Hey pal," said Neroy. "I, ah, heard that this was the place to come if you were interested in wildlife."

The butcher flashed a toothless smile, and gestured to the main display. A carcass that looked like a cross between a kangaroo and a porcupine was laid out in artfully arranged slices that gave the impression the unfortunate creature had been segmented where it lay, then presented on a bed of purple moss. Looking at it made Neroy feel suddenly nauseous again. Just like before, something inside him was starting to *twist*. Neroy took a hold of the display case and pressed on. The butcher glared at him suspiciously.

"Uh... yeah," Neroy said. "Actually, I was hoping for something... a little special." He paused, breathing deeply. It didn't make him feel any better. Neroy took out a fistful of local currency and leaned in over the counter, lowering his voice. Holding it together was starting to become a struggle. "Got anything to

Neroy smiled and emptied his pockets...

do with Raknaks? I was hoping to feed one, actually...”

The blackness in his gut twisted *hard.*

Neroy tried to scream, but couldn’t make a sound. Couldn’t move, couldn’t breathe—but he could still see.

The butcher’s face had melted.

No. It hadn’t melted, it had been flayed, along with the rest of his body. The butcher was screaming at him, skinned alive, his scarlet face a dripping mask of agony. The animal on the moss was thrashing too, each segment somehow alive again but capable of feeling only pain, only torment. All of the dead flesh in the shop was contorting now, chunks of tortured flesh everywhere he looked, with nothing to do but agonise. Then the laughter began, evil laughter everywhere, mocking their pain, taking delight in it, cherishing it. And it was hot now, scalding hot, the heat building up in an instant until it was everywhere. Inescapable. Unbearable.

Then darkness came, and took it all away.

Secure bioLab facility, Earth

Fenris wrinkled her nose in disgust. The flaking blood on the surgical table was days-old, now. Her blood. As soon as it was clear the procedure had failed, she hadn’t let them waste time cleaning up. Instead, she’d immediately deployed the technicians to research possible workarounds. New approaches. And that initial re-focusing had sustained her; helped her push past her immediate frustration. But now she was slumping.

Because she had to accept the experiment had failed. Again.

But she had been so sure, this time. It should have worked. An implanted womb populated with a baseline clone of herself, hybridised with just enough human DNA to create something new, but still compatible with her immune system, something her rigidly-engineered system wouldn’t reject. It should have *worked.*

With a snarl, she grabbed the surgical cyberArm closest to her. Digging her fingers into its metal carapace, she exerted her full strength. Her muscles went rigid with the effort. The technicians around her nervously backed off as the cyberArm started to shake. It should have *worked.* This time, the stupidity of those around her should finally have been overcome. This time, the maternal urge which had grown and grown inside her over the terrible, lonely years since the others had left her should finally have been assuaged.

It should have *worked*.

The end of the metal arm snapped off. She threw it as hard as she could at one of the organ tanks, shattering the reinforced glass and unleashing a grey tide of amnioFluid that swept across the Lab floor, carrying an assortment of artificial flesh with it.

Calm descended as Fenris' rush of fury dropped away. Repairs would need to be made, and new equipment obtained. She scanned the technician's reports again. One of them had already come up with some intriguing new research data on gene resequencing that might, possibly, provide the basis for a workaround. There was no theoretical reason that such an approach wouldn't succeed. But was that really enough to justify a whole new research programme?

Briefly, she considered how arbitrary someone else might see her efforts as being. How they might think that such a rapid new direction was ultimately a distraction, a justification for activity, any activity, that might possibly allow her to believe she could still advance her goal, rather than admit the possibility of defeat. She considered the perspective, then swiftly rejected it. With a conscious effort she deleted the thought.

Turning to instruct her team, she noticed that Taarbeq was hovering nearby, conspicuously failing to clean up the mess to which his colleagues were now attending.

"You are not helping the others," she stated. "Why?"

"Ah, I have that intelligence update you requested, Ma'am. On Elder Griffin, of the Candrassian Order. I would have produced it earlier, but the gene sequencing research you prioritised has-"

Fenris initiated a rapid dataLink transfer, cutting Taarbeq off as his synapses suddenly became very busy. She snorted dismissively as the information flooded into her. There was little of value, given Taarbeq's shoddy data management capabilities. But it appeared that Griffin was putting a team together, for an offworld operation. That in itself was unusual. When they used to work together they'd moved from System to System, but for the last ten years he hadn't left Earth.

Ever since the incident had occurred.

What had Griffin called the place where it had happened? *'A cursed orb'*. That was it. She snorted again. Religious nonsense. But still. That far out, beyond The Systems, the situation they'd encountered was... challenging. And the solution that Griffin had found. How had he referred to it? *'A terrible sacrifice'*. But from her perspective, he'd acted with atypical efficiency.

Given the circumstances as he'd described them to her, killing all of his colleagues—save one—had been the only way out.

Although he had never given her more than an outline of what had really happened. She had remained onboard the ship, keeping it ready to depart. And when a crazed Griffin had returned with Sphinx, half-dead, the story of a malevolent alien AI, and an Elder Citadel containing functional alien technology had been tantalisingly high-level. Then Griffin had snapped out of it, they'd raced back through the Link—and EarthFed had fallen apart, with everything that followed on from that.

Still, despite his seemingly rapid recovery, Griffin appeared to have been affected by it. As one would expect from a human. Since then, his priorities seemed to have become more focused. Which had sometimes necessitated the running of errands on her part, in exchange for his continued patronage.

Indeed, the occasion of just such an errand had been the last time she'd seen him. There was some extra security she'd been required to provide at a bar run by the Order, very discreetly, in the Peach Heights district. A local gang had started gravitating to it around five years ago, following a gambling incident and a subsequent fatality involving one of their members. Matters had threatened to escalate to a level that the barman, despite his enhancements, couldn't handle on his own. So she'd taken care of it. Since then, she'd assumed all had been quiet.

Fenris dismissed Taarbeq and looked around the Lab. Had she been made somewhere like this, originally? Given the circumstances of her discovery, it was impossible to know, now. In that moment she hated her unknown makers with a passion that stirred her emotions to a rare level of intensity. Her last ten years in the wilderness had been truly horrible. Not that she'd really felt it. Not consciously, anyway. The constant thrashing against limits that couldn't be broached, a painful inability to grow as she wished, driven by the desire to be free. To change.

To no longer be alone.

The hatred faded to irritation, the emotional cascade stabilised, and Fenris returned to planning. She quickly reviewed the research team's files. The gene resequencing would require a walk-in cauldron chamber to provide the necessary operating environment, to deconstruct her DNA sequences by using very high temperatures to break down skin samples. Such temperatures needed to be precisely calibrated to avoid permanently cooking the flesh of the subject, based on the specific properties of their skin. Hers was more resilient than most. Lost in thought, she raised a pale hand in front of her face. The calibration process was apparently an extensive one, given the need for recovery time after each initial scouring session. The procedure was both intricate, and painful.

There was no time to waste.

De'Spyr, Mu Draconis System

The heavy *chuk* of metal biting deep into wood woke Neroy with a start. He was tightly restrained, but managed to twist his head in the direction of the impact. The first thing he noticed was the butcher had his previously-melted face back on. The second thing was that the metal object was an enormous meat cleaver sticking out of the bed-sized chopping block he was strapped to.

"Ah, you've sharpened it enough now," said a voice. "So let's get on with it. Some guy comes in asking questions, has a seizure, then passes out? Might as well put him to good use..." Its owner walked into view, another evil-looking guy in a blood-spattered white apron.

Neroy raised his head to look down the length of his body. As far as he could tell, none of the blood on him was his. But that might not remain the case for very long. His head was clearing rapidly now, the fog of recent unconsciousness lifting, leaving a desperate fear in its wake. Not any kind of strange psychological terror, or hallucinatory dread, but a very clear and simple fear of dying an agonising death. And the worst of it was that it wasn't anyone's fault but his own. With street skills this rusty, he had no one to blame but himself. What the hell had he been thinking, walking into somewhere like this without a backup plan?

"L-listen guys..." Neroy began, but trailed off. He couldn't think of anything more to say.

The two men looked down at him, and the one he'd spoken to before smiled. He still didn't have any teeth. "Shh," he said, putting a grimy finger to his lips. "It'll be quick, I promise." He raised the cleaver to the ceiling, shifting his weight to his back foot in preparation for a decisive, downward stroke.

The butcher's head exploded in a spray of bone and brains, and a spear grew out of his friend's chest.

Rough hands freed Neroy and pulled him up. It was the Vizier and his men. Neroy sat on the edge of the chopping block, trying to find something to look at that wasn't covered in blood, human or otherwise. He gave up and stared at the floor for a while, watching the dark claret from the butcher's neck-stump slowly pool around the Vizier's feet.

The Vizier passed a leather flask to Neroy. It was the good stuff he'd had back at the Palace. Neroy drank deep, nodding his thanks. The Vizier scrutinised him closely. He must have detected signs that Neroy was basically unscathed, because he then became very angry.

"Idiot!" he snarled, dismissing his guards to the front of the shop. He paused until they were out of earshot. "I told you we would discuss where the Raknak meat comes from in good time. And we would have done! But you wouldn't wait. Instead, you end up here, in a place you shouldn't be, asking questions that almost got you killed!"

"...and from there to the belly of the Raknak, right?" Neroy held out a hand and the Vizier passed back the flask.

"Indeed. A supply chain of which the Princess is currently unaware. And will remain so. Hence the need for utter discretion."

Neroy frowned. "Ah, the Princess doesn't exactly strike me as the sensitive type. Why-"

The Vizier grabbed the flask and stuffed it back in his robes. "Her Royal Highness doesn't need to know, because Her Royal Highness also doesn't need to know that her consort-before-last accidentally ended up on the butcher's block after spending the night in a thoroughly disreputable tavern, and then an even more disreputable whore house, where no one knew who he was. Unable to settle his debts when due, the proprietor took payment in kind."

Neroy blinked, suddenly nervous. "Why are you telling me this? If you don't want Princess Alloria to know."

The Vizier shoved his face very close to Neroy's. "Because if the Princess is presented with the facts of the matter, by you, then she will subsequently be presented with convincing evidence, by me, that you are, in fact, an agent of her brother's, acting with the aim of facilitating his claim to the throne."

The Vizier drew himself up and made ready to sweep away. "And if that were to happen, Mr Sphinx, the Raknak would be the least of your worries."

Sitting in his room later that night, Neroy finally drank enough to stop wondering what the hell the meat vision had been all about. De'Spyr was so screwed up, it was surprising he hadn't started hallucinating the moment he'd landed. He poured one last glass and checked the worldNet device again. The trade ship was still due tomorrow, the first of a week of scheduled arrivals, so whatever had disrupted the flow of offworld traffic must have eased. He lifted his dinner tray off the bed and put it on the floor in preparation for turning in. Not a bad meal, for which he was thankful. Tasty selection of root vegetables, and some kind of local pasta analogue, albeit a little furrier than he was used to.

But the meat he'd left untouched.

The late morning sun angled deep into the Princess' study as Neroy was ushered in by a burly pair of guards. They bowed and left, closing the door behind them. The throne room had been heaving with soldiers, twenty at least, hyped up and ready for trouble. Every eye had been on him as he'd passed through with the Vizier, and none had been friendly. Neroy pushed it from his mind. He was on a timeline now, just about ready to go. Everything he'd bought at the Bazaar was there, ready and waiting, but his attention was on the bandolier of stuffed money pouches the Princess was holding.

"Half a million creds, Mr Sphinx. Fifty per cent upfront, as agreed."

Neroy took it with a grateful flourish, and checked the door. Still firmly closed. "I never doubted it, Your Highness. I am most honoured that-"

"Yes, yes, enough of that," sneered the Vizier. "We're sure you are. More pertinently, we're dying to know exactly how you're planning to use all of this equipment." He affected a look of austere disapproval. "Some of it was rather expensive, you know."

"Now, now, Vizier," smiled the Princess. "I'm sure Mr Sphinx knows what he's doing. Don't you, Mr Sphinx?"

"Oh, indeed, Majesty," said Neroy. He tied the bandolier around his chest, and walked over to where the equipment was laid out. Whoever had arranged it had done a good job. The chamCloak was draped over a mannequin to one side of the room, with the other items arrayed on shelves behind it, so everything could be easily viewed and accessed. The consort-skin bag had been moved from its hiding place, and was hanging from a nearby wall hook. A pair of leather gauntlets dangled from an adjacent peg, presumably intended to protect the Staff from his filthy offworlder's touch.

Everything he needed was ready.

Go.

Neroy pointed above the fireplace. The Vizier and the Princess needed something engaging to look at while he talked, to distract them properly. "If you could pull back the drapes, please, we can run through the plan. The map will help to clarify the details, Your Highness."

Princess Alloria opened the curtains, then stepped back to get a good view of the Labyrinth.

Neroy gestured to a point on its left edge, as far away from him as possible. "The first thing we need to take care of is in that entry chamber, on the Western side."

The Princess and the Vizier drifted over, the Princess' eyes screwing up as she tried to make out every detail.

"What's the point of that, then?" she demanded, already sounding annoyed.

Neroy licked his lips. Her attention span was even worse than he'd anticipated. Luckily he'd decided to start the walkthrough with a bang.

The Vizier lowered his voice to a stage whisper. "Perhaps he's thinking of accessing the maze through the dungeons… they were flooded last year, you know, and he has a breatherMask…"

Neroy reached for the equipment shelf. He cleared his throat, holding out the breather he'd picked up as his small audience turned around.

"Sure do," confirmed Neroy. "Best that money can buy." He slipped it over his face and sealed the filters. As the Vizier's jaw dropped, Neroy tossed the stun grenade he was holding in his other hand over to the Princess. It landed at her feet. She looked at the purple gas coiling up from it with an expression of utter confusion, before slumping to join it on the ground. The Vizier lasted a couple of seconds longer. He managed to stagger as far as the mantelpiece before collapsing. As he did he snagged a heavy lamp and it fell with him, smashing loudly on the stone floor.

There was an instant knocking on the door.

With no one to answer the guard's enquiry, Neroy knew he only had seconds. First the chamCloak. He scrabbled it on and activated it, then fumbled for the jet pack. Putting it on under the cloak was awkward, but he snapped the harness shut just as the door opened. A guard's head appeared around it just as Neroy realised he didn't have the glass cutters. Too late to risk it now.

Then the guard's jaw slowly started to droop as he took in what had happened. He hadn't raised the alarm yet, so Neroy changed his mind and stuck his arm out from under the concealing folds of the cloak to grab the cutters. On instinct he took the consort-skin bag, too.

He had no need for the Staff, but screw the Princess.

The guard roared for his officer to join him, so loud it made Neroy jump and almost drop the bag. More guards piled in to the anteroom. In an instant they were surrounding the Princess' inert form. Neroy crept to the open door undetected, but a scrum of guards waited outside.

There was no way through.

Neroy stepped to the side in case anyone else decided to rush in. There was a small stool by the wall. Neroy stood on it to raise himself above the guards' eyeline. No one was facing in his direction. Everyone was looking towards the fireplace, and the Princess. Neroy took a stun grenade in each hand. He activated each one by touch, then tossed them into the throne room, aiming for the far corner. A moment later a gratifying number of guards thudded over. The nearby soldiers hurried to investigate.

It was the only opening he was going to get.

The door to the clockroom stood open on the far side of the throne chamber. The path to it was clear. Neroy didn't hesitate. Moving as quickly as he dared, clutching the cloak around him, he crept silently across the room. Seconds later, he was through the door. The little waiting room was quite empty. As Neroy crossed the floor, he cast a quick look at the gilded clock on the table. The mummified skull at its centre looked just as despairing as before. As he passed it, Neroy couldn't resist giving it a quick nod of acquaintance. He could use all the friends he had right now.

Neroy hopped up on to the couch under the window, the volcano in the distance seemingly smoking a little more than before. Taking out the glass cutters he quickly glanced behind, but everyone still seemed focused on the stunned guards. The window was huge, made of reinforced glass designed to stop a sniper's bullet. But the glass cutters were industrial-strength. There was no time for subtlety, so Neroy cut a crude square out of the bottom of the window. It didn't take long, and then there was nothing to do but brace himself.

Things were about to get very noisy, very fast.

Neroy thumbed the chest control of the jet pack and waited until he could feel the engine thrumming in standby mode. He reached forward and rested the palms of his hands on the sides of the square segment he'd just cut out. A deep breath, then he pushed hard. Neroy didn't hear the glass smash on the cobbles below, although he knew it must have been loud.

As a mild breeze reached out to flutter the edges of his cloak, Neroy shuffled through the hole in the window and crouched awkwardly on the outside ledge. He could hear everything now, the songs of faraway birds, the mowing of a distant lawn, and, directly behind him, shouted commands and the pounding of booted feet on stone floors as the guards burst into the clockroom.

Then he punched the control stub on the jet pack, and the ledge fell away as the sky reached down and hoisted him up.

The jet pack was almost out of fuel by the time Neroy neared the Landing Ring. The haptic feedback pulses had quickened to a thrumming tattoo of warning as he dropped further and further down, the higher elevations he'd initially travelled at now completely unobtainable.

A final descent began, a shallow glide that the pack's programming was enforcing based on its dwindling power reserves in order to prevent a sudden, more terminal descent. He'd been following the road from the City, but before he was able to sight the Ring, he'd dropped further down to a level below the forest trees, now shielding his destination from view. The empty grasslands below sped past in a blur of green and brown, cut through by the grey streak of gravel that the road became as it approached the primitive spaceport. A final cluster of trees lay dead ahead. Neroy banked to avoid them, bringing the Ring into view.

It was empty.

Fear seized him as he pointlessly scanned the area around the Ring, but there were no ships to be seen. According to the landing schedule, the first trader should have arrived an hour ago, but something must have gone wrong. Imagining an angry crowd already setting out from the City gates to lynch him, Neroy coaxed a final, sullen increase in speed out of the pack. But he lacked the fuel to get any further. And even if he had been able to travel on, he had no other destination.

Neroy cursed the impulse that had made him snatch the Staff. The Princess needed it back, as quickly as possible. If he'd left it behind, she might have cursed him and then become distracted by the urgency of the task at hand. But now? She'd scour the face of the planet for him. Neroy had almost reached the Ring when the ride suddenly became turbulent. For a heart-stopping moment he thought the fuel had finally run out, and the jet pack was stuttering before finally switching off. He was still a hundred metres above the ground. Far too high to survive.

A thermal wave slammed into him from above, as a fast-descending ship fell towards its landing point.

Neroy angled down towards the side of the Ring, steepening his descent. He swooped towards the small cluster of maintenance buildings, a huge dung-heap coming into view behind one of them. He touched down next to it with a surprisingly gentle bump.

Seconds later the trader ship landed with a blasting howl of super-heated air. But as its engines idled down, the turbulence continued. A second ship was falling from the sky, closely followed by a third. Neroy shrugged off the jet pack and threw it into the dung heap, followed by the Staff. They both sank into the moist brown sludge. Then he remembered to power-down the chamCloak.

A cry from behind made him spin round, reaching for a stun grenade.

It was the boy he'd met before, down on his knees, shaking in terror. Neroy realised how it must have looked when he'd turned off the chamCloak, suddenly popping into existence from thin air.

"P-please don't take my soul!" stammered the boy.

Neroy shouted to him, raising his voice to cut through the noise of the landing ships. "Your name's Bozz, right?"

The boy nodded, terrified.

Neroy removed the breatherMask. "You remember me, right? The traveller, from before?"

The boy gulped and nodded, then rose unsteadily.

"Listen," said Neroy, lowering his voice as the noise from the ships abated. "I need your help, Bozz. Real bad. Those three ships on the Landing Ring—do you know them? Their captains?"

Bozz nodded slowly. "Y-yes, milord. They are all regular traders."

Neroy smiled, as charmingly as he could. "Which one's the least successful? The most in need of money? The one who strikes the worst deals?"

Raising a shaking hand, Bozz pointed out the smallest of the ships, an ancient, battered shuttle. A landing ramp was slowly extending from it. Neroy reached it in seconds, jumping onto the ramp before it touched the ground. The airlock was open now, and a startled-looking trader was starting to emerge as Neroy reached the door.

The woman snatched-up a weapon from her belt and pointed it at Neroy. But following a swift and efficient exchange of information, and the passing of the bandolier from Neroy's hand to hers, she lowered the gun and opened a comm link to her captain. The ramp began to slide back in to the side of the ship, and the engines, still ticking as they vented their excess heat, started powering up again.

Neroy sighted Bozz lurking by the dung heap. He waved at him energetically, hoping to get his attention in the seconds that remained before the airlock door closed.

"Hey, kid!"

Bozz looked around, then caught sight of Neroy. He cut a pathetic figure, in his rags and bare feet. Poor kid. What was it the Princess had said? *Only commoners can seize the Staff at any time.* Well, Bozz surely qualified for that lowly rung on the social ladder.

Neroy cupped his hands around his mouth and shouted against the engines' rising howl. "I didn't give you a tip for your help just now—so here it is! None of us wants to shovel shit forever, but you should keep at it…"

Neroy stepped inside the airlock as the door began to slide shut.

"…you never know what you might dig up."

The terrifying appearance of the torture chamber was only slightly diminished by the fact that the Vizier was seeing it all upside-down. Princess Alloria had ordered him chained to the wall with his head pointing downwards, as was tradition for those advisers blamed for a catastrophic failure like Sphinx's betrayal. Blood rushing to the head was believed to reduce the rate of bleeding from the feet, which was where his flaying was to commence, thus—theoretically—extending the duration of his imminent agony.

The Vizier had been hanging suspended for hours now without anything happening, which was absolutely fine with him. He had no illusions as to the likely outcome of the Princess' wrath. However, his still-loyal aides had sent him whispered updates throughout the afternoon, and, based on the wild rumours rippling towards Xaancholi from the direction of the Landing Ring, an extended preamble was very much in his favour at this juncture. All he needed was sufficient time for rumour to solidify into facts on the ground, and his fortunes might yet be transformed.

A harsh shout came from the corridor, followed by a scream.

The Vizier tensed. If the Princess had decided to clean house while she still could, there was nothing to be done. Not for the first time that day, he wished he had followed his mother's advice and become a spice trader. But a calling for public service had always been his curse.

The door flew open and a sobbing Constanz was dragged into the cell by his hair. The Vizier relaxed, as much as he was able.

"Save me, cousin!" screamed Constanz, sighting the Vizier.

The Vizier sighed. "I rather think I require some saving myself, at this juncture."

The guards chained a weeping Constanz to the wall and swiftly departed. On reflection, the Vizier felt they'd seemed nervous.

That could be a good sign.

"Do compose yourself, Constanz," said the Vizier. "Your mewing makes it impossible to think."

"What good is thinking going to do?!" wailed Constanz.

"Whatever its limits, thought is all that is left to us right now." The Vizier gently rattled one of his chains against the wall. "Action, for now at least, seems precluded."

The Vizier must have blacked out for a time, for he was suddenly awoken by the door crashing open. Even upside-down the Princess looked as striking as ever, her features marred only slightly by the desperation that twisted her face into a grimace.

"I may be about to die, but I shall have the satisfaction of seeing you two skinned alive before I do!" she screamed.

"Am I to take it that rumours of the Commoner-King, new wielder of the Staff, have proven to be true, Majesty?" enquired the Vizier.

"Bozz is his name!" she screeched, snatching up a red-hot poker from a brazier. "And I shall brand it into your face before I tear off your skin!" She pointed at a quivering Constanz. "As for him—guards! Castrate this fool!"

Constanz, beyond terror, could only moan in despair. But underlying his groaning, another sound was washing in from the corridor now, like the roaring of the ocean.

"A moment, Majesty, before our much-deserved punishment commences. I propose a trade," said the Vizier.

Princess Alloria advanced the poker to within an inch of the Vizier's nose. The heat was ruinous.

"What could you possibly have to offer me?" she spat.

"A way out," said the Vizier. The roaring from the corridor was louder now. "From the sounds of it, a crowd has stormed the palace. Law and custom dictate that when they find you, you shall be boiled alive to provide the stock for the new King's coronation soup."

"First I'll have the satisfaction of seeing you-"

"It needn't come to that, Majesty."

"What are you talking about? The law is clear-"

"The law only applies if they catch you, Majesty. At the other end of this corridor lies the throne room. Just beyond it lies the entrance to a concealed passage leading to the Forest of Zarn. Let me live, and I shall tell you how to access it."

"Tell me now, worm! Or I shall-"

"Torture me? Forgive me, Princess, but weren't you going to do that anyway?"

The roar from the corridor had risen to the point that the Vizier had to shout. "Best hurry, Princess Alloria. Fate favours the swift." From his inverted perspective, the Vizier could see the guards had fled. Vibrations from hundreds of running feet were starting to shake the room. The Princess glared at him with a look of utter hatred, then dropped the poker and ran to the door.

"Where is the passage? Tell me!" she shouted desperately.

"The anteroom where Sphinx briefed us," called out the Vizier. "Stand in front of the fireplace and twist both candleholders to the right—then jump into the aperture that appears!"

With that, she was gone.

Moments later, a ragged group of wild-eyed peasants burst in. They stared in horror at the instruments of torture, but hovered on the threshold, uncertain.

"Friends!" shouted the Vizier, with great passion. "Free us! The Princess wanted us dead to prevent us from aiding the new King, as we are known sympathisers of the common man! She hated the love we have for those such as yourselves, and the support we pledge to King Bozz!"

Spurred on by his words, the commoners enthusiastically released the Vizier and his cousin. As they staggered to their feet, Constanz dropped his voice to a shaky whisper.

"What are you talking about?"

"But what of the Princess? Might she not still do us harm?"

The Vizier smiled. "Not from inside the palace furnaces, which is where the ash shaft terminates. Quite a vertiginous descent, as I recall." He clapped a peasant on the shoulder in a comradely manner. "They never stop burning," he explained to his cousin, "as the palace kitchens require a constant source of heat." The Vizier beamed, a twinkle in his eye. "It rather seems the Princess will be assisting in preparations for the new King's coronation feast, after all."

CHAPTER 6: INTERSTITIAL

Candrassian Order Mother Temple, Earth

Clarence Griffin fought the urge to gag at what he'd just seen. Odysseus, Lead Operative on the mission despatched to Proxima one week previously, had just made contact. Odysseus' ship had emerged minutes previously from the Sol System's Gateway, and he'd immediately established a sharedReality link.

Griffin was seated in the Mother Temple on Earth, and Odysseus was millions of kilometres away. But the sR headset Griffin wore made it seem like they were in the same place. A bland, vaguely-defined corporate meeting room. One of those places that could have been anywhere, and in this case, literally was. Lying beside Odysseus, immobile in a medical bed, was Acolyte Lamai. Griffin had recognised her severe black hairstyle immediately, and kept his focus fixed rigidly on that feature now, to prevent him from looking at her face again.

It had been burned beyond all recognition.

Thankfully, she didn't seem to be conscious.

"What happened to Acolyte Lamai?" Griffin asked.

Odysseus glanced at her, then adjusted a black medical device attached to her torso. "She was making enquiries in the Proximan underworld about your Mr Sphinx." Odysseus' tone was completely flat. "As you may recall, the Order is rather unpopular on Proxima. Her cover was blown, and she became involved in a confrontation with hostile elements. One that involved the use of thermal grenades."

Griffin forced himself to look at Lamai. Her hands were the same as her face. Red-raw and shiny, like the melted shell of some unfortunate sea creature.

"She will receive the best medical care the Order can provide," said Griffin, acutely aware of how inadequate his words sounded.

"Of course," dismissed Odysseus. "But in any case, it was all for nothing. Sphinx wasn't even there."

Griffin sighed deeply. Fajid, Azrael, Lamai. Once again, others in the Order were suffering. Just as before. The guilt of his terrible sacrifice, ten years ago, would always be with him. The deaths of his companions. Necessary to stop the darkness, but nevertheless. Deaths for which he was responsible. Griffin's doubts started to rise. Perhaps he should involve other Elders, rather than just seek operational support from juniors like Lamai. Perhaps...

No. He didn't need other Elders.

He needed Communion.

Griffin paused the sR link, the walls of the Cloister Nest instantly solidifying around him. He closed his eyes and let the physical reality of the Temple retreat as he slipped loose his mind. Griffin gave in to the constant whispering at the back of his head as he allowed his spirit to commune fully with the Loving Essence of those around him, and with those in the City outside. And beyond that, even, to the very edges of the Order's network of Earthly believers.

Communion, that balm for the soul that every adept within the Order could fall back on in times of spiritual challenge. Communion, a technique available only to those select few who had mastered it. Nothing to be used lightly. Already he could feel its siren pull tugging at him, hooking into him, whispering at him to stay.

But no. He was needed. There was much work to do.

Griffin opened his eyes, bolstered and restored. The guilt was quite gone. The events of a decade ago? He'd done what he'd had to. It had been a terrible time back then, which gave him every reason to stay in control now, especially regarding Neroy, with a renewed threat rising. Neroy. The key to it all.

He reactivated the sR link. Instantly, he was back in the meeting room. With relief, Griffin saw that Lamai had gone. Odysseus continued with his report. Sphinx wasn't on Proxima. Eventually, intelligence reports had picked up his trail on some hideously-backwards planet, and from there he'd been tracked to Deneb IV, where other Candrassian operatives had managed to take remote psychometry readings whilst following Sphinx on the planet's Orbital.

At last, thought Griffin. Something solid to go on. Odysseus transferred the data to him, and he reviewed it quickly.

"Excellent," smiled Griffin. "The intensity of his nightmares and hallucinations is increasing. Just as I'd hoped."

Odysseus glowered. "Forgive me, Mr Griffin. But Lamai briefed me on Sphinx's... condition, based on what she was told by yourself." His tone hardened. "Why was his memory not restored immediately, so he understood his role with us? His current nature... has resulted in this unnecessary pursuit. One which has already proved most costly."

Griffin shook his head. "No. The horror of his past must be drip-fed, for to receive it all at once would overwhelm him. His true character, his missing memories, must re-emerge slowly, naturally, as he emerges from his cocoon and re-acquaints himself with the methods of his guileful trade. Clumsy interference would risk distorting his personality—rendering him useless." Premonitions, Signs, Portents. They had all pointed the same way over the years. Neroy was an essential part of any possible solution.

Precisely how, though—that, still, was unclear. All Griffin felt he knew for sure was that Neroy himself must be preserved. And that had to mean restoring him to being the man he was before. Interference in his character and nature could ruin his suitability for whatever lay ahead. It was a risk Griffin simply refused to countenance.

Odysseus looked ready to argue but continued his report, concluding that Sphinx had been unaware of the presence of the Deneb IV operatives, but had moved planetside before they had attempted to secure him. Griffin was about to end the meeting. But then Odysseus offered a final, grudging update. Disturbances were occurring in the Kumeiijm'a System. Reports were tentative, confused. But ships had been reported missing, and strange rumours were beginning to spread.

Griffin thanked Odysseus and closed the link. Slowly, he removed the sR helmet. Dark Shapes flitter, he thought. Heading our way along the Great Link and out into the Kumeiijm'a System, from the source of the ancient evil.

He looked up at the spindly-legged artefact in its case above the Cloister Nest, the one poor Fajid had passed when all this began. He could have accessed the sR link from anywhere private, but this had felt like the appropriate place.

Since the incident with Fajid, everyone in the Temple had been giving it a very wide berth.

Fajid. Azrael. Lamai. And now Odysseus, too, seemed resentful. It occurred to Griffin that his operatives might lack the necessary effectiveness for the task at hand.

Some hours later Griffin was still working in the same Cloister Nest. He heard tentative footsteps approaching, then a handsome young woman started descending the stairs to join him.

"Acolyte Cornell!" said Griffin, rising to greet her. Relatively new to the Order, Portents had indicated she may be of some minor use. "Thank you for answering my summons so quickly. I have an urgent errand for you, here in the City."

"Ah, uh, of course, sir," replied Cornell.

"Please don't be concerned," Griffin reassured her. "I'm not sending you to meet anyone dangerous."

Cornell nodded quickly. "Who am I looking for, sir?"

Griffin smiled. "Fenris. Her name is Fenris."

CHAPTER 7: WHAT YOU SEE AIN'T WHAT YOU GET

Deneb IV, Tau Ceti System

Neroy yanked hard on the iron shackles, but they were fixed tight to the chair. He could raise his arms a couple of inches, but that was it. The chair was metal, and cold, and he'd started shivering as soon as the cops had strapped him in. He looked down at himself. Naked aside from his underwear.

It was a depressing sight, so he gazed around the interrogation room. White tiles covered every surface, with a black circular drain in the middle of the floor. At the room's edges, grimly functional pieces of equipment lurked, all shining blades and vicious little drills that would look unpleasant enough in a hospital.

But he wasn't in a medical facility.

A stretch of time passed, then an old-fashioned key rattled loudly in the door. A fat, deeply unattractive man waddled in. He brought with him the sound of a woman screaming somewhere, the sound of it bouncing around the tiles until the thick cell door closed. Agent Bukowski was aggressively overweight, the kind of smug cop who wore his belly as a badge of honour. He didn't need anyone to like the look of him, or even like him at all. He was more than fond enough of himself.

"OK, Sphinx," he sneered. "Let's see you get out of this one."

Bukowski stopped to examine a complex piece of apparatus, rolling it away from the wall. It was multi-armed, each articulated limb ending in a different kind of cutting implement. Neroy forced himself to breathe deeply. The trick was staying calm. Bukowski had certain expectations. So it was all about meeting them.

Just stay focused on the prize.

Bukowski looked up from the machine and smiled. "Things certainly seemed a little brighter this morning, didn't they?" He snorted a piggy little laugh. "But then again, we hadn't really gotten to know each other properly. Had we?"

Neroy hadn't wanted to wake up that morning.

The Emperor-sized hotel bed had been way too comfortable, and the night's friendly gymnastics had left him fuzzy-headed, and a little sore. But he'd roused himself when he'd heard the girl padding across the carpet of the Master Suite, heading for the room service terminal. It had felt way too early for more champagne, but the perfect time for something stronger, like some of the local brandy he'd already developed a taste for.

The girl hadn't been wearing a stitch, and neither had he. She'd turned and smiled at him across the room, gaze all sultry, just like she had the night before when they'd met at the City Museum. He'd been at the Museum to check out the Imperial Flame, the largest diamond on the planet. She'd been flirtatious, then bold, and then, back at the hotel, inventively enthusiastic.

That had been the night before. And now that morning had come, it was time for refreshments. When she'd reached the menu terminal she'd turned her back to him, and he'd had to search out her expression in a nearby wall mirror. Her lip had suddenly curled, then the air around her had started to shimmer as the room went cold. The edges of her form blurred and distorted, like a transmitted image suffering from interference.

And then she had *changed.*

In one obscene instant her supple flesh had bloated outwards as her frame expanded in every direction. Rolls of fat had bloomed under skin that lost its tan to become white and hairy, her limbs had stretched out, her feet and hands expanded, her hair had shortened and then, as her head's facial features melted into a new, much less pleasant configuration, her gender had also changed.

But the smile had stayed the same throughout.

The obese nude man had introduced himself as Agent Bukowski. Before Neroy had had time to do more than pull on his underwear, a squad of riot police had stormed the room, arrested him and dragged him to the door. The unclad Agent Bukowski had remained mostly silent, but what little he had said to Neroy had been spoken into the mirror, and he hadn't turned around.

For which Neroy had been profoundly grateful.

Agent Bukowski adjusted a barbed drill on an interrogation unit, humming to himself. Neroy watched him closely. Bukowski seemed a proud man, on the surface. But there was a seam of inferiority beneath it all.

"All that trouble for me last night?" Neroy said, aiming for a tone of brittle confidence. "Prepared to do just about anything for your planet, weren't you."

Bukowski stepped back from the machine, giving it a little pat, as though it was some kind of loyal pet. He drew himself up with a pompous flourish. "I am prepared to make any sacrifice for the security of Deneb IV." His face took on a gloating expression. "But then of course, you had no idea. How could you have? Our morphTech is so refined these days, don't you think?"

Neroy slumped. "It... I... no. You got me, pal. I had no idea who you really were. None at all. But how did you *do* that? I never came across tech like that before, anywhere..."

Bukowski puffed out his chest and began strutting around the cell, like a pudgy cockerel. "No, of course you haven't. And yes, it is an intriguing ability, isn't it?" He paused, giving Neroy a quick once-over that positively shouted *there's no harm telling you, you're never going to be leaving this cell.*

Neroy looked down at the chains binding his body. From this perspective, it was hard to disagree with such an assessment.

"As remarkable as it must seem to you, it's essentially a shapeshifting technology," boasted Bukowski. "Don't ask me how it works on any detailed level. As you may have noticed, the transformation's accompanied by a change in temperature and atmospheric composition within a two-metre radius. It seems to strip-mine organic molecules from one's immediate surroundings, or dump excess mass as required, based on initial body form."

Keep on stroking, thought Neroy. "But-but how the hell..."

"Apparently it works along related lines to a portal," Bukowski responded airily, humouring his subject. "It uses a variant on teleportation to stretch, compress or distort bones, organs and all the rest of it. *Detachment and reassembly*, I believe they call it." He patted his ample belly. "The device is surgically implanted. It intertwines with one's nervous system, mapping the baseline body on a molecular level, and the AI control system's fed a 3D scan of the target form."

"Does... does it hurt?" asked Neroy. He couldn't stop a note of hope from shading his tone.

"Not at all," dismissed Bukowski. "It suspends your pain centres during the transformation." He paused, shrugging. "It does, however, place a great strain on one's metabolism, so I won't be using it again any time soon." Bukowski patted his stomach again. "But then, now that I've got you, I won't be needing to."

He drew out a small tablet. "It's the cream of the crop from our R&D teams. Exactly the kind of thing Deneb IV is fully capable of. Did you know, we were actually more advanced than your people when the Earth ships arrived? But we always lacked a sufficient industrial base from which to challenge you." His nostrils flared. "Well, that's all going to change, Sphinx! And sooner than you might think! Admittedly, we only have a few prototype devices at present, but its use was amply justified to snare such a valuable asset."

Bukowski lifted the tablet to his nose, and began to read. *"An intimate conversation where one party is uninformed as to the other's true identity is often the best way in which to extract crucial information, or gain their confidence to distract from an upcoming manoeuvre...*"

He lowered the device, and smiled. "The Denebian State Security Procedural Manual is a constant source of good advice, Sphinx. You confirmed your criminal nature to me beyond doubt, and you were completely defenceless when the snatch team grabbed you."

"Mind if I borrow that manual when I get out of here?" Neroy asked. "Sounds like a guy could learn a lot from it. Although given how excited it seems to make you, I guess some of the pages might be stuck together."

Bukowski flushed a deep purple. He seized an arm of the interrogation device that ended in a scissors-like double blade, and shook it angrily in Neroy's direction. "You think there's a way out of here for you, Sphinx? Believe me, when I get started, you'll beg to tell me everything!"

Neroy drew a choking breath. "Yeah... I guess a guy like me, with my rap sheet... all those arms deals I pulled... you were always going to grab me..."

Bukowski snorted. "Please! No, you're a second-rater at best. Your criminal record is of no interest to me. But we're not stupid, you know. An S&M man turns up, you don't think we're going to react?"

Neroy leered. "S&M? Last night was steamy, I admit. But I played nice..."

Bukowski flushed. He grabbed Neroy's chin in his chubby hand. "We know you were an officer in EarthFed's Supply Management Directorate, Sphinx! It may have been a dozen years ago, but what you know could be invaluable to us."

Neroy's world stopped. The diamond was what he was after here. What the hell was Bukowski talking about?

He tried to process what was going on, but all he could do was sputter. "W-what?" A piece of his past, from within the Cold Black Glass. What the hell was going on? "But... I thought... my interest in the Imperial Flame was what—"

He managed to shut himself up. Keep control of your reactions, then take it from there. Amateur. Stupid amateur. He was better than this.

But goddamn it, Bukowski had started talking again. The dumpy asshole was strutting around the room, busy warming to some new theme.

"...of course, economically, EarthFed was always thinly stretched. But the needless inefficiencies! Knowledge transfers were limited to maintain the status quo. But what happened as a result? A Ponzi Scheme economy, no less, on an interstellar scale! Swindling Arcturus to bribe Sirius, as it were. Ore from here, to buy food from there, to compensate for energy theft elsewhere. And you were part of that, personally, for years!"

He stared at Neroy with something like envy. "It must have been glorious, Sphinx."

A cloud passed over his face, and he returned to his monologue. "But it didn't work, did it? Too much waste, corruption. Too much value, leaking out of the system. But those artefacts-from-before, Sphinx. Gifts from the ancients, whoever they were. They kept it all going for a while, didn't they? What little innovation there was, fuelled by tawdry offworld excavations. Stripmining ancient facilities. Panning for flecks of gold amidst the ruins..."

He trailed off, lost in thought.

Neroy laboured to pull himself together before Bukowski veered off on some other topic. He'd clearly been right on the money in using Bukowski's interest in the military complex as a way of getting his attention. But the apparent connection Bukowski had just made with Neroy's hidden past was a total wildcard.

"Supply Management... sure, I've heard of them. Don't remember working for them, though..."

Bukowski glared at him. "We *know* you did!"

"Didn't say I didn't." Desperately Neroy tried to think of an angle, but all he could muster was to be direct. "My memory these days… isn't what it ought to be. Sounds like you know more about it than I do. So why don't you spill the beans…"

"Cut the crap, Sphinx," snarled Bukowski. "We've got you dead to rights. A man with your record goes to the same museum for three days in a row, it isn't in pursuit of self-improvement. You were after the Imperial Flame Diamond." He shrugged. "Not that I care about that, as such. But nevertheless, the facts are what they are." He leered at Neroy. "And, as of now, they're my facts."

"My record?" said Neroy. "Now, what would you boys know about that, all the way out here?"

Agent Bukowski drummed his fingers on his gut, with a suddenly agitated tempo. "EarthFed may be gone. However, we still have close ties to Terminus City. But not close enough. Weapons technology transfers have slowed to a crawl. And it's not exactly a friendly universe these days. We're accelerating our defence research, but we're always playing catchup. Earth could turn hostile anytime."

He grasped his hands behind his back, and bent over to look Neroy in the eye. "That's where you come in. We need dirt. Backdoor passwords, blackmail material—anything to give us some leverage with Terminus City."

Bukowski smiled, doing his best to look sincere. "If you help me, there's still a way out for you, Sphinx. Just work with me here."

Neroy couldn't help himself. "Work with you? Now, Agent Bukowski. I thought we were, you know... closer than that. Don't tell me you were faking it last night."

The interrogation device must have been right behind Bukowski, because suddenly the blade-tipped arm was in his hand.

He leaned in slowly, and carefully snipped off Neroy's thumb.

Two weeks before the nude man in the hotel room, Neroy had been lounging in a bar on De'Spyr Orbital. Like most Orbitals it was a freezone outside planetary jurisdiction, its security forces prioritising the commercial interests of the owners, the Independent Customs Authority that ran a string of Orbitals along the trade route from Earth. The only ship departing for weeks was heading for Deneb IV.

Neroy had sat there, reviewing options. When he'd left Earth, he'd wanted time to think. To figure out what had happened to him, in a place nobody would be looking. He'd tried that on De'Spyr, somewhere behind the back of beyond, and hadn't gotten anywhere. Except almost killed.

But Deneb IV was a hi-tech world at the heart of things. Unlike De'Spyr, there'd be records he could access. TC was off-limits because of Dubblz, even if he could have gotten there. So Deneb IV would have to do. He'd need to steer clear of the authorities, who had a reputation for paranoia. But the way things were going these days, he'd thought, who could blame them? Because rumours were definitely starting to spread. About something grabbing ships. Out near Kumeiijm'a, of all places. The place where his memories resumed. As he'd considered it all, it hadn't felt good. And the fact that his memories restarted at the point when something had caused The Fall of EarthFed? That hadn't felt good, either.

Maybe, he'd thought, he'd find something on Deneb IV to tie it all together.

The *Empress of Sol* was a BioTransport Colony Support Ship for the few isolated outposts Earth had left. Headed for Idris Prime, its next stopover had been Deneb IV, and there was more than enough room for a paying passenger. It was a hulking vessel, a miniature world with a range of distractions for crew and passengers, but in the course of the ten-day journey Neroy often found himself in the bowels of the ship, with the livestock. They were interesting to look at.

The ship's core function was to be an interstellar seed bank, putting together bespoke DNA packets of baseline flora and fauna to sculpt the ecospheres of Earth's client worlds, in whatever directions might best meet the current requirements of interstellar agricultural trade. Most of the biostock was in stasis, but a proportion needed to be ready for deployment. Over two hundred worlds across the former EarthFed harboured a seemingly-endless variety of alien animals, most of which appeared to have ended-up in the ship's crowded lower reaches. Never intelligent, but that was the only constant as far as Neroy had been able to tell from gazing at them, in their cages and tanks and vivariums. That, and the fact that all of them had been selected due to a commercial value of some kind.

WingSquids, with their tentacled beaks, produced antibodies that oncologists would kill for. Altarian Slime Devils were regenerative, with the added bonus of being compatible with human nervous systems, making them an invaluable source of organ transplants and guinea pigs for medical devices. Although their putrid green colour and creepy feelers that stroked languidly at the air, like the half-hearted caress of a feeble lover, really got under his skin. And Flesh Petals—pink blobs covered with sphincter-like orifices, whose extracts were apparently useful for those with psychic abilities.

Neroy had befriended the Chief Keeper, a hard drinking old coot who'd taken to him for some reason. They'd share a bottle as she fixed the day's broken equipment at the end of every shift. She was an engineer at heart, one of those people who think best with their hands. Some of the creatures they controlled with meds, but the toughest ones needed cybernetic chips, mannequin implants that allowed a human controller to literally take over the animal if required. Given the precise tasks some of them had to perform in the labs they'd been bred for, AI wasn't always enough. The implants allowed a controller with a headset to literally see things from the creature's point of view as they made them do whatever they wanted, filtering out any unpleasant sensations that might overwhelm the controller.

The thought of it had disturbed Neroy when the Keeper told him about it. You'd have to be pretty desperate to want to experience the world as a Flesh Petal did.

Neroy had been of the firm opinion that one sphincter was quite enough.

Deneb IV's Orbital had been similar to De'Spyr's. In the shuttle on the way down, Neroy had been undecided as to whether he'd look for a job, or continue on with the *Empress*. As the shuttle curved into the atmosphere, entering the range of the planet's satellite network, Neroy's dataLink had flared into life. He'd spent the rest of the descent soaking up information. Elements of Deneb IV's society had always been on a par with Earth's, and some of its pre-EarthFed technology had even been superior, but it lacked a large population base, and was currently dominated by a paranoid, authoritarian government.

There had been evidence of that at customs. Some poor sap had been dragged off screaming. A discrete check of the dataFeeds had clarified that the planet's security service had a terrifying reputation, and weren't gentle with prisoners.

All the more reason not to get caught, he'd thought.

Capitalis City had been pleasant, full of green high-rise spaces and dune-like structures that undulated in subtle wave formations. Neroy had gravitated to the City Museum. The Denebians placed great store in their planet's natural wealth, culminating in the reverence shown to the Imperial Flame, asserted multiple times in the Museum Catalogue to be the Largest Diamond in Existence.

And it wasn't just how big the Flame was, he'd learned. It was what could be done with it. According to the Denebians, it also had unique energy-amplifying properties. Neroy hadn't been impressed with the claims being made for it. According to the Denebians, it was the Biggest Diamond in the Galaxy.

But it wasn't even the largest diamond he'd stolen.

However. It had been right there in front of him, and by the time he'd left the Museum he'd known he couldn't pass it by. Sure, he'd screwed up a little on Earth. And also, to be honest, on De'Spyr. But he'd felt that it was nonetheless time to get to work again.

He'd had a real good feeling about this one.

Neroy's severed hand lay on the tiled floor of the interrogation room like a withered piece of meat. Bukowski's white-hot blade had cauterised the stump instantly, so there wasn't much blood spatter.

Neroy tried to count the crimson dots, but lost track after the first half dozen.

He was overcome by a fundamental sense of disassociation, an out of body feeling that made it very hard to focus on what was happening in the room. He knew there was pain somewhere in his system, a tidal wave of it, but it was flowing somewhere else for now. Suddenly he felt very far away indeed. He forced himself to concentrate on what had just occurred. After the thumb, he'd insulted Agent Bukowski again. It hadn't gone down very well. Then the bone saw had come out, for his hand. It was shocking to have a piece of your body cut off like that, to see it lying there, detached from you.

He shuddered. Bukowski was prepared to do anything to learn more about Neroy's Supply Management days. But Neroy had nothing to say, despite being intensely interested himself. A revelation from his past was the last thing he'd expected to find in this room, but he had nothing on the topic to offer Bukowski.

He looked at his hand on the floor and shuddered again.

Bukowski snapped his fingers. "Now now, Sphinx," he said. "I appreciate you're feeling a bit of a shock. That's understandable. But I'm afraid it's going to get rather worse, rather quickly. Unless you have something to tell me..." He rolled over another piece of equipment, this one with a snaking attachment that ended in a small, circular spin blade. He pressed a control and serrated segments, like a series of tiny shark fins, popped up around the saw's circumference. "Access codes. Decrypt sequences. Anything you can tell us from your S&M days. Or I remove one of your eyes, in a way no surgeon can ever fix."

Neroy had nothing to give.

"You know, you really aren't what I was expecting, based on the psych profile in your EarthFed records," Bukowski said, folding his arms. "Oh, they're a decade and a half old, but still. Core personality traits shouldn't change that much. But you're... well, less arrogant. Warmer." Bukowski adjusted something on the apparatus. "Ah well," he sighed. "It should make you easier to torture, in any case."

Bukowski took up the spin saw and gave Neroy's eyes a quick inspection. "The left, I think. We've rather neglected that side of your body so far." He paused, with a smug little smile. "Oh, and just so you know? The joke's on you. The Imperial Flame? You were only ever checking out a fake. The real one's being used in our Las-Weapons research, at the Planetary Tech Institute. The Museum? It was never even there..."

Neroy managed to summon a scream just before the saw bit into his face.

On his second day on Deneb IV, Neroy had done some research. Security at the Museum was impregnable, so he'd focused on people. Weak points. What did they need, that they didn't have? The Head Curator, he'd discovered, always wore gloves. To hide the fact his little fingers had been cut off by mobsters he owed money to. Bad gambling habits will do that, Neroy had thought. Especially to bad gamblers.

On his third day on Deneb IV, Neroy bought his way into a card game with the Curator and his creditors. Cleared the man's debts, taking information in return. The information had been unexpected, and only went so far, but had clarified the next part of the journey. The Imperial Flame on display was a fake. The real one had been taken by an Agent Bukowski for weapons research, given its unique properties. However, nothing was recorded digitally. Deneb

IV was a paranoid State. Constant bureaucratic infighting. To avoid hacking by his enemies, Bukowski carried it all in his head. So Neroy had looked into him, mapping Bukowski's wider network. For a way in.

Then, as ever, he'd found one.

Bukowski had been spending a lot of time with a Professor Trjakian. Who, based on her recent publications, was in an inter-world research network with a certain Professor Carver, famed portal specialist from TC, back on Earth. Carefully, Neroy had used Dubblz's access codes for Carver's portal project, still stored in his dataNode, to review Trjakian's project files. Trjakian, it had emerged, was working on something rather interesting.

Neroy's prowlerWare was swiftly kicked out of the research network, but the private medical database he'd then moved on to, detailing Trjakian's narcotics issues, had barely needed hacking at all. When Neroy had visited her, he'd been able to tell just by looking at the woman. Addiction like that must have made it far easier for Bukowski to control her. But that cut both ways. Neroy had found her at her lab, along with the tech he needed. She hadn't resisted, especially with the candy he'd brought.

After that, Neroy just needed some way of snagging Bukowski's attention.

There wasn't any reason for Bukowski to be interested in him that Neroy could think of, so he'd had to spice himself up. Make himself bait, then go fishing. He'd added a fake criminal record on himself to the police database, with a focus on museum thefts to make it crystal clear what he appeared to be after.

Trjakian had told him all about Bukowski's MO by then, and how to detect the man. She'd also clarified his obsession with offworld weapons tech, so Neroy had added a few fictitious arms deals to his record, to bait the hook. Adding things to a criminal record was never the hard part. It was taking them off that was sometimes the challenge in life. Then he'd returned to the Colony Support Ship to prep the final elements. He'd developed a good relationship with the Chief Keeper, and knew the woman's appetites well by then.

On his fourth day on Deneb IV Neroy had returned to the Museum, where he met a beautiful woman.

Neroy's vision cut out completely for a minute. Then it eased back in around the right side of the room, but the left was a sucking void. The remnants of his eyeball were smeared around a surgical tray on top of the torture machine. With surprise, he noted the absence of even mild pain. He hadn't noticed being drugged, but Bukowski must not want him passing out. The thought of pharmaceuticals interfering with his cognitive patterns made him briefly panic, but then it passed. As far as he could tell, everything was still working the way it should.

Time to go for it, while the cue from Bukowski was still in the air.

Neroy hacked up some phlegm and drooled into his lap. Nice and pathetic. He'd have started crying if he could, but he'd never been much good at that. Pity, really. Sadists like Bukowski really got off on stuff like that.

"Oh Gods… the Planetary Institute... can't believe you guys had it there the whole time..."

Bukowski laughed, delighted. "Hah! It's not even guarded! Just tucked away in the basement testing area, with the crystal samples."

Neroy went slack. His head lolled slowly to one side as a short moment turned into a long one, and then another. Drool began dripping from the corner of his open mouth onto his chest, mixing with the long, red smear that ran down from his ruined eye socket.

Dimly, very dimly, he was aware of Bukowski's voice from a long, long way away.

"...gone a little quiet..."

"...no shame in it..."

"...sooner or later, you'll..."

"...not a patient man..."

"...Sphinx?"

Neroy snapped open his remaining eye and grinned at his interrogator.

Bukowski leapt back, dropping Neroy's chin as though he was suddenly holding a hot coal.

"Sorry about that," smiled Neroy. "Been a little busy. Shuttles don't land themselves, you know."

"Guh!" Bukowski exclaimed, eyes popping.

Neroy looked down at his ruined body, as his outline began to shimmer in the suddenly frosty half-light of the cell.

The *change* was seconds away, now.

Bukowski shrank back, aghast.

"Well, can't say it hasn't been fun," grinned Neroy. "But I've got things to do..."

Speech would be beyond him very soon, now. But not quite yet.

His hands were becoming tentacles, pale skin sliding down the spectrum to a septic green as his undergarments split, torn apart by a thrusting array of spikes and armoured plates.

Bukowski threw up his hands. "Wh-what..."

...the left was a sucking void.

"The Altarian Slime Devil you can keep, pal. Although without the control unit for its mannequin implants, you'll find it a little hard to keep in line. But I'm told they taste pretty good, if you can get past the smell."

As Neroy's vision faded, the last thing he saw was Agent Bukowski vomiting copiously.

Neroy relaxed, relinquishing control.

In that final instant, he sensed another mind sliding into the body's driving seat as he vacated it. As he left, he forced out one last, halting sentence. "morphTech... is so refined... these days... don't you think?"

Neroy cut the connection. The duality with which he had been moving through the world resolved itself back to a single sensory track.

The inside of the shuttle came vertiginously into focus as the overlaying view of the cell cut out. Hands shaking, Neroy tore off the control headset. He rose from the padded bunk for the first time in a day, and grabbed a bottle of water. He was stiff as a board. The Slime Devil's temporarily human-looking body was the only one he'd been moving since he'd started controlling it remotely twenty-four hours ago, seeing what it saw, speaking through its animal throat, but feeling only a tiny, edited fraction of its sensations.

As he drank, Neroy rubbed his temples. He cursed the BioShip's Chief Keeper. Damn headset was way too tight, and he'd been wearing it all day. The woman knew her stuff, but she must have the tiniest head known to humanity. He tossed the thing out the window as the shuttle touched down outside the unobtrusive grey sprawl of the Planetary Institute. As soon as Bukowski had identified it, the shuttle's AI had plotted a course and then hovered at a distance, but now he knew exactly where the Imperial Flame was. There was no time to waste.

Bukowski. Technically, he'd never actually met the guy, and Neroy was keen to keep it that way. By now he was probably scanning the poor Slime Devil, and once he'd found the morphTech implants and the mannequin control at the base of its brain stem he'd ride the control frequency back to the headset's last active location. Which would take him straight to the Institute. But by then, Neroy would be safely back on the Orbital.

Hopefully.

He stumbled out of the shuttle into a light rain, grabbing his kitbag on the way. The equipment in the bag should still have some juice left from De'Spyr. Almost fifty percent when he'd checked, a few days back. The prowlerWare his dataLink had sent ahead had done the trick, and a side door slid open as he staggered through the drizzle. It wouldn't last, but he had a temporary secure route right through the place, straight to the testing area.

The splash on his dataLens showed a temporary blind spot form around him, a spherical null zone slowly rolling through the Institute, alarms and sensors all turning a blind eye as he descended to the basement. This late at night, the place was deserted. As he moved, his thoughts slunk back to Bukowski. That kind of enforced intimacy was hard to shake off immediately. And how he hated that goddamn smile. Weird how the girl had smiled like that too. That kind of smugness must be more than skin deep. Even if Professor Trjakian hadn't told him how to scan for Bukowski's implants, that smug goddamn smile would have told him who to look out for back at the Museum.

Neroy shook his head as he moved through the Institute's gloomy interior. Bukowski would soon start fading away, he knew. But the S&M revelations were here to stay. Because they made sense. S&M sounded like they would have been a central part of EarthFed's Military-Industrial Complex. They'd have had the ability to doctor records. And maybe alter people's memories. So now he had a candidate for the insertion of the Black Glass into his mind.

Thinking about where the Glass had come from made him suddenly realise he'd reached an accommodation with it. He wasn't trying to push through it anymore, and it wasn't pushing back with headaches and nausea. But the question of why it was there would have to wait.

Because he'd reached the basement.

Neroy focused on the sensation of conditioned air moving across the backs of his hands as he let everything but the job slip away. He took the chamCloak out of the bag and pulled it on. Still on standby, but there if he needed it. Suppressing passive alarms was one thing, but reaching out and taking something? That could well trigger a more resilient system. The crystal samples were all lined up in a single display case running the length of the lab. He'd been concerned the Flame might be hard to find, but it was twice as large as the next-biggest rock.

It was a beautiful thing. Obviously unique, now that he could see it for real. In the murk of the basement an enchanting fire danced within, a shimmering glitter that seemed to reach beyond its outer surface and sparkle in the air. Gently, he reached out and touched it. The uncut stone was smooth, with a hint of static that made his fingertips tingle. It was practically unbreakable, but he grasped it tentatively in both hands and ensured his balance was steady. Then—slowly, carefully—he lifted it up.

An ear-splitting alarm went off.

A shout cut across the shrill of the alarm, then another guard answered the first from somewhere closer-by. All he had to do was activate the chamCloak and he could slip away, he knew he could. There was still time. Just.

But the darkness that had suddenly arisen inside wouldn't let him. Then the darkness *twisted*, deep in his bowels, and the glitter of the diamond in his hands became a septic, dripping fire that flowed down his arms and engulfed him, swallowing him whole until all the world was aflame, impossibly hot and impossibly painful, melting every part of him in a way that left him entirely present, to endure and suffer on. The laughter didn't start—it had always been there, he knew that now—but it intensified, its delighted mockery making the pain even harder to endure. On one distant, meaningless level, Neroy knew the experience had only begun seconds ago.

But already it felt endless.

Secure bioLab facility, Earth

Fenris scowled through the cauldron chamber's reinforced porthole at the idiot waiting outside. The woman looked young, barely more than a child, standing awkwardly in the middle of the laboratory where Taarbeq had left her, over an hour ago. Fenris tutted. The scouring session was almost over, and already the temperature inside the chamber was dropping to a level close to something a baseline human could survive. For brief periods, and only if they were unconcerned about irreparable brain damage. But from the looks of the fool waiting outside, that was unlikely to be much of a loss should it ever happen to her.

She checked her skin samples were secure, and activated the opening sequence. The safety overrides insisted on an internal temperature of less than 104 degrees before the door would open. She glared at the locking mechanism while she waited. Then the indicator turned green, and she thrust the door open.

The idiot yelped in surprise, stumbling backwards as Fenris emerged, steaming, from the cauldron's flame-red interior. There was a console behind her. The fool toppled over, sprawling on the floor in a puddle of cooling fluid that had leaked from the cauldron seals. The gloopy blue liquid quickly stained the trousers of her light grey leggings. A Junior Acolyte's habit, Fenris noted with irritation.

"Why didn't Griffin send someone more senior?" Fenris demanded, crossing her arms. "Were you the only one available?"

Acolyte Cornell picked herself up, grimacing as the coolant fluid seeped more deeply into her clothes.

"Um, sorry, ma'am," she apologised. "Elder Griffin felt it would be sensible to minimise data-based communications. So he sent me. To, uh, invite you to join a sharedReality session with him." She nodded swiftly. "At your convenience."

Fenris stared down at Cornell. She was deeply unimpressive. But presumably that meant she was also expendable. Not that Griffin would allow himself to see it that way. The human capacity for self-delusion never ceased to vex her. Especially his.

"It's about Sphinx, isn't it?" Fenris waited briefly for a reply, then continued. "Hmph. Of course it is." However irritating it was, she supposed she'd have to talk to Griffin. Earth authorities were increasingly paranoid, and she required his continued patronage.

"Very well," she said, grudgingly. "I shall contact him." Sphinx, she thought. It was almost certainly to do with him. Annoyingly, she felt a tugging at her thoughts in the direction of the past, their past, a tugging that then re-directed itself towards the future. A future that might once again contain the structure they had worked within before. The group. Their group. An efficient, productive arrangement within which she had-

No. She had no interest in Sphinx or Griffin. Not anymore.

The Acolyte seemed less nervous now, peering curiously around the laboratory.

"Ah, I was wondering, ma'am," the Acolyte said. "What exactly were you doing in there?" She pointed at the cauldron. "I've never seen anything like it."

Fenris stepped aside, smiling. "Feel free to inspect it for yourself. I'm just about to start another cycle."

Deneb IV, Tau Ceti System

Neroy shuddered as the room snapped back into focus. He couldn't move, couldn't even think. The sonic assault from the alarm was drilling into his skull, driving out everything else. He staggered and almost fell. Two armed guards were running towards him from the other end of the lab, shouting words he couldn't hear. He limped away from them, lugging the diamond and looking desperately for somewhere to hide until he remembered the cloak. Fumbling one-handed for the controls, he managed to activate it as the guards were reaching for him.

He only just made it to the shuttle.

The Mulch Pits by the animal enclosures were the best place on the BioTransport Ship to get rid of something. The combined effluent from all of those incompatible digestive systems was utterly toxic, and as soon as Neroy tossed the chamCloak into the bubbling slurry, the damn nuisance began to dissolve.

Good riddance. Because once again, he'd discovered he was rustier than he realised, just when he'd needed to turn it on. The thing hadn't had half a charge, it had barely been on ten percent by the time he'd activated it back at the Lab. He'd started flickering into view before he was even halfway out of the Institute.

Although it was a miracle he'd had the presence of mind to use it at all, given the hallucination. He'd managed to avoid dwelling on that during his escape, as the return journey had demanded his full attention. But now...

Neroy forced his thoughts back to the Cloak. There had been no sense in hanging on to it, it was dead, and he had no way of recharging annoying, artefact-derived tech. Nobody outside of the military would have the right equipment for that, the technology was just too esoteric compared to the commercial stuff everyone else used. Who really knew how something like that was powered, anyway? But however it had worked, it was incriminating. And now it was useless. Neroy watched as its remains sank into the Mulch, releasing a cloud of foul-smelling gas. He wrinkled his nose and strolled off towards the animal pens.

The remaining Slime Devil was female, according to the Chief Keeper. Whatever its gender, the thing wasn't happy on its own now that its mate had disappeared. It was slumped morosely on the ground, surrounded by droppings and a scattering of half-eaten food. Neroy's stomach wasn't feeling too good after the Mulch Pit, and he leaned against the guard rail that surrounded the enclosure.

The creature must have sensed something, for it raised its head, scanning slowly from left to right until it saw him. As soon as he did, it locked onto him.

A deep fear gripped Neroy as the creature stared right at him.

Then the odd sensation in his stomach *twisted* and the world dropped away, plunging him into a place of terrifying, impenetrable darkness. Wherever he was, he was alone, lost forever, aside from the terrible presence behind him. He didn't dare turn around, even though he knew exactly what it was, and what it would do to him.

And then the Devil was in front of him. Not just the creature from the Ship, although it had the same form, but a real Devil. A demon, an obscene tormentor, a bringer of agony and humiliation. The laughter was there in the darkness, cackling gleefully as the creature slowly ate him alive, each second stretching out in an eternity of unbearable pain. It felt like it would go on forever. Even the very concept of it ending seemed inconceivable. He had always been there, and always would be.

Until suddenly he wasn't.

Just like at the Institute, the transition was instantaneous. One second he was being devoured, the next he was staring at the Devil slumped back down on the filthy floor of its pen. Neroy felt like joining it. He was spent, completely exhausted, clothes wet through with sweat. Hunted. That was the name for what he was feeling. Something inside him was waking up, hauling itself into the light by dragging him down into his inner darkness. It wasn't fully awake yet, but it was coming. OK. Think about it later. But not now.

Back in his cabin, Neroy fell into bed. Despite his exhaustion he popped a couple of pills to make sure, and sank gratefully under as the darkness came.

The Horror was there, waiting for him.

It was almost familiar now. The feeling of utter terror. The searing flames burning him. Unbelievable agony. And the mocking laughter twisting around the edges of the white heat that flayed him, blocking everything out except the pain. But then something else. Something he could somehow tell was new. There was another person there with him. Not a tormentor, not someone there to inflict pain, but rather another sufferer. A comrade. Someone he knew, but couldn't remember. A man. A man screaming, just as he was, but somehow as much in fury as in pain. A man with dark, ebony skin, reaching out his hand to Neroy, almost as though he could save him. Almost as if there was a way-

Neroy woke up screaming so hard he couldn't breathe.

Once he'd calmed down to the point that there was nothing left except a wretched, lingering fear, he realised he'd just experienced more of the same nightmarish hallucinations as before. Whether they came at night, or as waking dreams, they were building up now, more harrowing every time. But what it meant and where it all was heading, he just couldn't say.

The *Empress of Sol* had a dozen bars of varying levels of comfort, but the quality Neroy required was proximity. The nearest bar to his cabin served alcohol, and it was open, and after that there weren't any criteria that mattered.

A third of a bottle of rotgut later, and his dataLink had spent enough time nosing around Deneb IV's dataWeb for him to have learned a little more about S&M. Not much, but it definitely sounded like something that would have suited his skills. Somewhere in a secure database he couldn't find, let alone access, was all the data Bukowski had on him, and his past. But it might as well have been on the other side of the galaxy.

What was it Bukowski had said? Dubblz had made the same observation. That he was less of an asshole, now. Warmer. Not so arrogant. Neroy smiled. He must have been quite the guy, back in the day. Then he felt a surge of frustration. There was just no quick way to access the information he needed. And he had to get moving. Now. Jurisdiction or no, Bukowski would be sending people up to the Orbital before long.

They could be in the bar already.

The place was getting busier now. A party of wealthy types trouped into the bar and huddled around a table at the edge of the room, clearly uneasy. Asking around, Neroy discovered they were refugees, but who or what they were fleeing from remained obscure.

People kept drifting in. Neroy started mingling, asking around and letting it be known he had money to spend on transport. The *Empress* wasn't due to depart for ten days, way too long to be safe. But as one conversation led to another, a new topic kept coming up. There was trouble brewing. Out near Kumeiijm'a. Some of the talk was wild, with speculation of privateers or some seriously screwed-up lost colony, out to cause chaos.

No one went so far as to suggest aliens, but it was clearly linked to what he'd heard on De'Spyr. Although this time there was no doubt that there was definitely some form of actual trouble, signalled by a dribble of wealthy refugees, and ships that were too slow to report back, or confirmed missing. As ever, inter-System communications were patchy, and came in packets, borne by the swiftest ships and the most talkative crews.

Rumours spread fast between Systems, hard news less so. But something was definitely up.

Starting in on a new bottle later that evening, the insight hit him. Not as a dramatic moment of revelation, but as a realisation after the fact. The S&M clue somehow related to Kumeiijm'a. He was suddenly sure that it did. Some kind of association that just felt right. Ice. A hospital. And the woman, the job they'd done together. Tall, blonde, clad in black. If she'd stuck around back then, they could have taken over that iceball planet together. He wondered where she was now, then shoved her out of his mind. No point dwelling on someone you're never going to meet again. Which, he swiftly decided, was almost certainly for the best.

There had definitely been something of the wolf about her.

But nevertheless, it felt time to retrace his steps. Aside from operators like Bukowski, any S&M information on him was likely to be in a dataVault in TC. He'd need to head back there at some stage. But not before he'd figured out a way of dealing with Dubblz.

The trader he showed the Flame to had a small, antiquated ship. But it was well maintained, and the man was willing to go wherever Neroy wanted. Kumeiijm'a. Things sounded like they might be a little hot out there. But no risk, no reward. The terror of the nightmare was gone now, drowned in the booze. But Neroy knew that wasn't the end of it. He needed to find out what the hell had been done to his mind. Memory blanks, dreams, hallucinations. Kumeiijm'a. Suddenly, he somehow knew that whatever had been done to him had started there.

CHAPTER 8: INTERSTITIAL

Candrassian Order Mother Temple, Earth

Fenris was utterly unchanged from ten years ago, Griffin thought, studying her across the table in the sR conference room. It was lovely to see her, it really was. Despite the fact that she looked ready to lean over and rip out his throat.

Her aggression was welcome, in a way. It helped him focus, pushing away the lingering remnants of the Vision which had seized him just moments before she had arrived. The involuntary Premonition had been brief, but awful. A hideous creature in a dark, frozen cave at the edges of which a fiery glittering whispered for his attention. A scurrying presence approaching unseen and then—rocks, falling endlessly, burying him alive.

Griffin curved his fingers through the air. The light pouring in through the virtual window dimmed to a dappled, late afternoon glow. He cleared his throat and forced himself to smile. "I'm sorry if I've taken you away from your research, my dear. I know how important it is to you." He nodded. "That's why I've always been so happy to fund it."

"Hmph." Fenris glowered, then crossed her arms in a swift, decisive movement that almost made him jump.

Griffin did his best not to smile again. She was a remarkable being in so many ways, despite her limits, and he had no wish to provoke her. "As I said, I'm sorry if I've disrupted your work. I'm very sympathetic to anyone who desires to grow. To become more than they are. Finding meaning in life is all that matters, in so many ways."

Fenris raised a pale eyebrow. "Indeed, Griffin. Given that, I presume you're still taking advantage of the beliefs of the credulous?"

Griffin gently shook his head. "Faith is not synonymous with stupidity, my dear. With all you've seen, you're in a better position than most to appreciate that, in many ways, what are seen as 'magic' and 'religion' are both true. Consider my own, modest abilities. A few centuries ago, I'd have been burned at the stake simply for being what I am."

"You're far too wily for that, Griffin. Which I've always found hard to reconcile with those pompous religious trappings you favour. Does your kind really still need prayers and temples?"

Griffin spread his hands. "From a certain perspective they are mere props, my dear. Necessary to amplify levels of Belief amongst my people. Even now, the prayers of the faithful fuel the abilities of myself and the other Elders. You simply can't obtain the necessary fervour from staff in a humdrum office complex, if you wish to generate sufficient... momentum... to tap into the Cosmic Forces that surround us. And more than that. When darkness is glimpsed, Glory offers balance to the faithful."

Fenris cracked her knuckles. "Whatever works for you, old man." She hesitated, then sighed as her body language softened. "He's back. Isn't he?"

Griffin shrugged. "Not quite. He's on his way. But I need you to help him get there. We all do…"

An odd expression flashed across Fenris' face. She quickly looked away. If Griffin didn't know better, he'd have said she was hurt. "You never did tell me what really happened back then," Fenris said. "Out there. Why he had to change. Why we had to disband."

Fenris' hand tightened into a fist. She stood up suddenly, knocking her chair over with such force that it hit the rear wall. Rather than bouncing off, the programme running the sR room made it disappear, instantly replacing it with another, identical chair that appeared just behind her.

"I need to leave now, old man. I have left an experiment running, that I must now return to."

"Please, my dear," replied Griffin, gesturing to the empty seat. "There's more you need to know. Based on our latest information, Neroy is now heading for Kumeiijm'a. Clearly, the universe is trying to tell us something. It's time to finish what was started."

Fenris didn't sit, but she didn't leave, either. She stood there, staring at Griffin with her dead, black eyes. Just right now, they didn't make her look frightening. They made her look empty, waiting to be filled.

"Do I have a choice, old man?" she demanded.

Griffin didn't reply until she sat down again. "Just as much as always, my dear."

"Hmph. So. Do you want me back on Kumeiijm'a?"

Griffin waved a hand dismissively. "Goodness me, no. Not after the damage you caused last time."

"Me?" Fenris snarled. "You were the one who almost killed him!"

"I was the one who saved him, Fenris," replied Griffin, coolly. "But in any case, ships have begun disappearing in the Systems close to Kumeiijm'a. Nothing dramatic, yet—but the implication must be that this is all linked to our debacle of ten years ago."

"Implication?" snapped Fenris. "How can you people not know for sure?"

"I realise you've always struggled to be accepting of uncertainty, my dear, but information flows between Systems aren't what they were. Current record keeping is often poor. Ships may not be missed for a while, System authorities don't want to be perceived as weak..."

Griffin trailed off. He placed his empty hands, palms-up, on the table. On that pre-set cue, the sR programme made a small wooden box appear within his grasp.

Fenris glared at it suspiciously.

"From the reports I have received," Griffin began, "Neroy will soon be ready for us to consider taking matters to the next level. He remembers nothing, I expect, but his nightmares must be hideous." Griffin slid the virtual box across the table. "The physical version of this box is being delivered to your laboratory. Prepare yourself to find Neroy. When the time is right, administer the contents to him—unseen—and then step back. He must become whole again soon, or all is lost. Humanity is depending on us. We need the real Neroy again..."

Fenris sat with her hands resting on the table. Griffin looked at them, noting her perfect alabaster skin, without a single blemish.

Distracted by something he couldn't quite remember, Griffin's attention shifted to the window. What was it?

"...oh, and speaking of your laboratory. Do you happen to know what's become of Acolyte Cornell?" Griffin studied the dusky light beyond the window as it swirled slowly, drifting and formless. "She really should have returned by now. Fenris?"

Griffin turned his attention back to the interior of the room.

But Fenris wasn't there anymore.

CHAPTER 9: ICE WOMAN

Ibn519, Kumeiijm'a System

Neroy walked out of the shuttle dome and immediately went blind.

Stabbing white light was everywhere, a squall of luminescence so intense it overwhelmed the senses on every level. He fumbled with the contrast on his suitVisor until his vision returned. The cold was harrowing, wind tearing into the exposed parts of his face like a spray of tiny arrows. It took another painful minute, but he managed to mould the fabric of his thermSuit's hood tight around his visor, until only his mouth was exposed. Snatching a breath of scouring air, he rose from the crouch he'd dropped into and turned away from the shelter of the dome wall, to face the City.

It was an absolute dump.

The planet had a serial number for a name, officially, but everyone just called it Kumeiijm'a, after the System's star, and that same lack of imagination extended to the name of its largest settlement. Kay-City was a sprawling company town, a settlement of black metallic structures pitoned to the ice that wrapped itself around the planet in a mile-deep layer, like pieces of an enormous, soot-stained machine that had been scattered across a frozen lake and nailed down to stop them from being stolen.

Humans had been on Kumeiijm'a for a couple of hundred years since the wormholes had reactivated, but the City still had an improvised, frontier feel. The whole planet was a company town in one way or another, run by a mining corporation that had implemented minor governance structures as a grudging afterthought. Everything was organised around drilling down through the ice, tearing ore out of the planet's buried crust and shipping it offworld.

The frigid hostility of the environment mitigated against society evolving to become richer and more textured. There were no farms, no tangential niches for rugged pioneers to occupy, no homesteads that could, over time, become villages then towns then cities that would eventually unlock the total dependence on mining. Everything here was about violating the planet, shoving the booty offworld and then doing it all over again.

Neroy clomped off down the bustling main drag leading away from the shuttle dome, slowly threading his way through the crowd. Everyone was swaddled in thick thermSuits, masked-up and silently focused on getting from A to B. On Kumeiijm'a, it was always about the destination, never the journey. It wasn't quiet—a backwash of industrial noise came from all around—but conversations were at a minimum. On Kumeiijm'a, people generally spoke indoors.

A rusty piton had been driven right into the middle of the road. Neroy stopped and gazed up at it. It towered over him, an enormous black harpoon that bit into the ground at a savage angle and carried on going for tens of metres. The building it anchored was a square, two-storey structure, like most of the others. In Kay-City, the real action was underground, in the warrens of composite-lined chambers that honeycombed the ice. The whole City was reconfigurable and movable, but it hadn't budged in decades. The ochre ore stains from the industrial processors surrounded the City for miles now, such was the richness of the local seams.

But the discolouration around Kay-City wasn't really so bad. One mega stain near the equator was like Jupiter's red storm cloud, the planet bleeding-out on a scale visible from space. Other blemishes he'd seen from the Orbital were curving lines, bloody gouges tracking the slowly-moving mobile mining cities. But from the rust on the piton, Kay-City didn't give Neroy the impression of being a place in a hurry to relocate. Which was a relief. He might still be able to pick up whatever tracks he'd left here, a decade ago.

A huge rust flake was close to breaking off the piton, but a twist of metal held it in place. Its stubborn resilience annoyed Neroy, and he was reaching out to tear it off when an angry hubbub broke out from the tethered building.

A bulky figure crashed through the window in an explosion of reinforced glass fragments.

He hit the ground with a crack, then slid towards Neroy over the ice, slowing to a stop on the other side of the piton. The miner's industrial thermSuit was composed of bulbous segments of black composite, like a swollen beetle shell.

He swayed to his feet, eyes rolling. The man lacked a helmet. Neroy could smell the stink of liquor on him from metres away.

Shouts rose as the door to the building was thrown open and another miner stomped out, moving as close to a run as his armour allowed. The two men slammed into each other with a dull clang. Both had uncovered heads, their cheeks starting to turn blue. Neroy wondered how they could see anything in the glare, but they seemed to be fighting by touch, each clumsily grasping the others' hands as they struggled to stay upright.

The man from the building managed to slip a hand free, and punched the swaying miner in the mouth.

The piston-like impact of the powered armour's gauntlet split the man's face with a soggy crack, like an axe biting into a log of green wood. The victor staggered back inside the building, where a segment of thick plastic was already being stretched over the broken window.

The corpse was left to freeze where it lay.

Even though the City hadn't moved, Neroy worried it might have reconfigured since he was last on-planet. The Bar might literally not be there anymore. But as he trudged on, the street layout seemed familiar. Being here was bringing it all back.

Over the past few weeks, bits and pieces of his previous time here had come back. A brief period of relative clarity and energy that had sputtered out as soon as he'd reached Peach Heights ten years ago, and sunk into a decade-long daydream. But with memories this close to the edge of the Black Glass, some of it had stayed hazy, and he'd been loath to push it. Headaches and nausea had taught him to treat the Black Glass with respect.

But now he was actually back here, everything was clear and sharp. Something about the place seemed to possess an extra depth. A resonance that stretched back through the barrier in his memories, feeling like a link in a chain that could haul him back to who he'd been before. Something he could take hold of, to help him get to grips with the visions, the nightmares and all the rest of it. Tentatively, he pushed at the Black Glass. Nothing. Yet. But being where his earliest post-Glass memories began felt like it had brought him right up against the memory barrier, in a way that was almost physical. Perhaps that would be the key to cracking its surface, or seeing through it, to whatever lay beneath.

For better, or worse.

The Bar was up ahead now. The only place in town that wasn't full of miners. Eccentric clientele, or what passed for it in Kay-City. Non-company types, independent operators. Even the odd criminal. It was the site of his earliest clear memories post-hospital, ten years back. He still had only very vague recollections of the hospital itself. No idea why he'd been there, or where he'd come from. Then things sharpened-up. A cheap room. The Bar. A woman.

It should be OK to revisit the place, though. Everyone he'd crossed back then should be comfortably dead by now, given what they'd all been into. Kumeiijm'a. Off the beaten track as much as a place could be. There wasn't likely to be any S&M intelligence here, lurking in a digital corner. From an initial survey, the rudimentary planetNet was either Mining Databases, or porn. His dataLink had little to connect to, and less to report back when it did.

But he was sure another angle would present itself, given the opportunity.

Neroy took a room in the habWarren under the Bar, then spent two days wandering around town waiting for inspiration to strike and freezing his ass off while it didn't. He hadn't recognised anyone from his previous visit, and nothing new had come back to him. There were a hundred and one angles to play in a place like this, easy scams he could run in his sleep—in a coma—and he half-considered them all during his rambles through every notable part of the City, his inner monologue like a corrupt tour guide's unspoken observations.

Chewing gum for the mind, but it wasn't what he was there for.

Then it was the end of the shift-week and a flurry of new arrivals blew into Kay-City like a blast of dirty snow, miners from outlying outposts, mixed with people who didn't like to hang around town any more than was healthy, but needed a taste of the Big City. For whatever reason.

He scanned the Bar as he sat back down at his corner table. The place was dark and crowded, and would have been cosy if the customers hadn't been so rough. He'd just sauntered over to the counter to pick up a fresh bottle, and to eavesdrop more closely on the most promising conversation he'd heard so far. An argument was brewing, though, and the woman's voice was now audible across the room.

"...ah, c'mon, man, can't you give a guy a break? I'm good for it." Her words were conciliatory, but her tone was barely polite.

The barman was having none of it. Bald, he had a hideously scarred face and a raw, grating voice. "You're at your limit, Yol. Settle up, or get out."

The woman kept on going. "Look, it's been a little tough, OK? I haven't been earning for the past few weeks, you know that. And you know why! It's not like I'm blacklisted or anything—it's the research. I'll be back at work next shift-cycle! But I've got to stay out there as long as I can right now. This place I've found—it's unique."

The barman laughed. "Yeah, I heard what you were telling those idiots just now." He jerked his thumb at a table near the door. "About the 'discoveries' you've made." He adopted a mocking tone. *"A lifetime's insights! In just five weeks!"* But you know what? It's a bunch of bullshit. I know you find stuff out there sometimes. Make a little money on the side. But really. Buried ruins, full of ancient secrets about hidden wormholes and what have you? I tell you this—our System don't have no 'second wormhole', but if you don't clear your tab pretty soon, I'll tear you one for free."

The woman simmered, but held her tongue long enough for Neroy to waddle over. His thermSuit was unzipped and on standby mode, but he still wasn't used to moving in it.

"Excuse me, friends," smiled Neroy, drawing a glare from both of them.

"What the hell do you want?" snarled the barman. "I'm in no mood for-"

Neroy beamed at them. "Well, firstly I was hoping for a glass of something warming. And secondly, I'd like to buy the young lady here a drink."

He nodded to her, earning a scowl. She had a strong, open face, a fierce intelligence in her brown eyes. Her features had an intensity that he sensed would be just as suited to conveying a sense of wonder, or fascination, or amusement, as they were to expressing her current look of brooding hostility.

The barman's eyebrows shot up, making the scars on his forehead dance.

...spent two days wandering around town.

"Her tab's over a hundred creds. You gonna clear that, too?"

Neroy dropped a small pile of credWafers on the bar. "Do you take money?"

Her name was Katyr Yol. Neroy bought her a beer, and she grudgingly agreed to join him at his table after a furtive exchange with her companions, which generated some unfriendly stares in Neroy's direction. She wore her thermSuit like a second skin over her solid, well-muscled frame, and as she strode over to his table, she moved with an efficient athleticism that stopped just short of being graceful.

Katyr dropped into a chair and downed half her beer, keeping her eyes locked on Neroy.

"You like Denebian brandy?" she asked, indicating his bottle. "Never met anyone who drinks that before. Little pricey for the local market."

"I've acquired a taste for it recently," Neroy replied. "And on this ice cube, I wouldn't drink anything else."

"Sounds like you've been here before."

"Just the once."

She leaned back. "Look, if there's something you want, can we get down to it? You cleared my tab, and I appreciate that. But I'm not here to make a new best friend."

There was a suspicious intelligence to her that suggested an honest, open approach was likely to pay off. Honest to a point, anyway. "No problem, Katyr. I appreciate directness. Saves time. So allow me to be direct in return. I picked up on a little of your earlier conversation, before I introduced myself. It intrigued me."

She opened her mouth, but he raised a hand. "If you'll indulge me?"

Katyr gestured for him to continue.

"Thank you," said Neroy. "Again, forgive my directness, but the tab I just cleared would take your average miner weeks to pay off. I'm not after anything specific in return—not yet, anyway. And in which case, who knows? Perhaps you've got another tab I can pay off. But in the meantime, I'd like to ask you a few questions. Then see where we go from there."

She didn't react in any positive way, but she didn't stop him either.

Neroy lowered his voice. "From what I heard, you've been doing some private research out on the ice. You found something, just recently. Something artificial. Something ancient. Something that—maybe—relates to the wormhole system, and Kumeiijm'a's place in it. Could you maybe tell me something more about that?"

At first she was reluctant. But, fuelled by a stream of the beers everyone in Kay-City favoured, and the opportunity to talk to someone who was actually interested in what she'd found, Katyr began to open up, once Neroy had used his status as an ignorant offworlder to reassure her he wasn't a company man, come to sniff out some prospecting violation.

"I've always been interested in history, you know? Runs in the family. My mother before me, her mother before her." Katyr's voice was thick, but still on the right side of slurring. "Real history, mind, not that crap the company teaches us at school to keep us all in line. Everyone thinks this place is a frozen, lifeless husk, but it wasn't always like that. Thousands of years ago, this place—it was occupied. And the people who were here, they left stuff behind. And sometimes I find some of it." She took a slug of beer. "Learn what I can, then sell it on." She looked guilty. "No one's paying me to find it," she protested. "I can't afford to hold on to it."

"You said 'people' just now," Neroy probed. "Were they definitely human? I've been around a little, lately. Seen some strange things. Like a wrecked ship I noticed up at the Orbital a few days back, before I came down here on the shuttle. It had damage that didn't come from any human weapons I know of. And there's a lot of strange rumours going around at the moment, too. Rumours pointing here."

She looked away. "Well, who knows?"

"I think you do, Katyr. Or at least you know something. I'd be interested in your sources, if nothing else. How exactly does a guy go about finding ancient artefacts, hidden under a mile of ice?"

"Whole planet's bristling with sensors. How do you think they find the ore seams? But the company's just following the money. If something else turns up, they're not interested. So sometimes the data gets passed to me, instead. No love lost between the Orbital scan team and the company these days."

"For a certain consideration, no doubt."

She flashed him a loose smile. "You got me. But really. It's nice to talk shop with someone for a change. Everyone else on this ice cube's either a miner, a hooker, or an engineer."

Two foaming beer tankards slammed down on the table. "Or a barman," grunted the bald, scarred man. "Gonna need a few more credWafers soon if you want to avoid another tab."

Neroy paid the man, then pushed both glasses over to Katyr. "Thanks, but no thanks. I'll stick to the brandy."

"Really?" queried Katyr, draining one of the beers and belching. "You never touch beer? It's all anyone here drinks."

"Not on Kumeiijm'a, my friend."

Neroy slowly poured himself a drink. Katyr Yol had something to her. Whether she was a dead end or not, there was something inspiring in wanting to know more about a hidden, unknown past, even if it was for ulterior, commercial motives.

Especially if it was for ulterior, commercial motives.

Neroy downed the brandy, wanting to fire himself up. So far, there was nothing to connect any of Katyr's activities to him, to his past. Except for one thing. It was something the barman had said, just before Neroy had paid her tab, that seemed to tie Katyr into his own personal timeline. It didn't make sense, as such, but he didn't need it to. Not immediately, anyway. There were too many pieces just right now.

But still.

"The barman said you'd been doing something for five weeks. Now what exactly did he mean by that?

She stared at him, then shrugged. "Well, it's true. Normally I fit short excavations in around mining jobs. Gotta pay the bills, right? But I'd been out there for weeks this time. Only came into town today to pick up supplies. Always more discounts at shift-end. You know? But, yeah. It all started five weeks ago."

Five weeks. As near as Neroy could calculate, that was when he'd woken up, for lack of a better term. Become himself again, before being snatched by Dubblz. The background noise of the Bar dropped away, and Neroy found himself staring at Katyr in a way he couldn't disguise.

"What started? Please, be as specific as you can."

"Well, uh, my guy from the Orbital sensor array. He gave me a heads-up about an energy signature they'd picked up in a mountain range near Kay-City. Right on my patch." Her brow creased. "But, you know, energy sources? Something active? That was totally new to me. They usually find stuff due to, you know, metallurgical scans, sonar pings, that kind of thing."

"Did they maybe have an idea what caused it?"

She looked like she wasn't going to answer, then did. "Yeah, maybe. Some kind of exotic particle stream's started up, flowing in-planet to that location from... well, from somewhere it wasn't coming from before."

"From the wormhole?" asked Neroy.

She shook her head. "Nope. Not the one we use, anyway. Who knows? Maybe it's got something to do with all those rumours of ships starting to disappear in-System."

Kumeiijm'a. The place where the Black Glass ended, and his memories began. Something had been activated here, simultaneous to his own reawakening, lightyears away.

He very much wanted that to be more than coincidence.

Neroy dropped a small cloth bag on the table.

Katyr stared at it suspiciously. "What's that?"

"Enough credWafers to pay for a hundred bar tabs. Or a second-hand shuttle. Or something else that might help you in your work. Or, hell, a ticket to Cassiopia for when you get tired of all this deep-freeze archaeology." He pushed the pouch across the table. "Your excavation site. Whatever it is, I'd really like to see it."

She looked uncertain. "Ah, I don't know... it's a long way out and, you know, I haven't completed the initial survey yet."

Neroy produced another bag, the same size as the first one, and dropped it next to its sibling. This time, Katyr looked inside. Then she quickly checked the other one as well.

"As a final sweetener, I'll pay the same again when we get back."

"OK," she said, quickly. "No problem. When do you want to leave?"

"Tomorrow morning."

"Why the hurry? It's not going to melt."

Neroy laughed humourlessly. "I don't sleep too well these days. Makes me kind of restless."

Katyr said she needed to leave to get supplies for their trip. He was about to try to persuade her to stay for another drink so he could ask more questions, when he saw the old guy walk in and start kicking the ice from his boots. It was someone from his trip here ten years ago.

Someone he very much didn't want to meet again.

Neroy had assumed the man would be dead by now, given what he'd been doing to himself back then. And he looked like he should be under the ice, with his cracked skin and vacant, milky eyes. Katyr registered Neroy's agitation at the man's arrival, but looked nonplussed. The nearest dropShaft was right behind their table, so after a quick confirmation of when and where to meet, Neroy was back in the habWarren and heading for his room.

Tomorrow threatened to be a long and interesting day. Neroy slept, and the Hell Dream was worse than ever. Fire. Agony. Mocking laughter, infinitely amused at his suffering. But again, something new this time, an extra detail that even after an infinity of suffering he just couldn't miss, despite senses awash with pain. The man who was suffering along with him was there again, but this time Neroy could make him out more clearly.

He was wearing a white suit.

It was just a tiny thing, but as soon as Neroy was able to grasp that detail amidst the torture of the furnace, he realised he was also aware of other things.

It was a place, a real place. A place of significance, of ancient power. They had entered through a door, a door he had opened, that he should never have touched. And around that door had been icons, sigils imbued with hints of dark and terrible meaning.

Twisted spiral> Burning sun>Broken pyramid.

Then everything span, sucked away into a dark tunnel that he plummeted down forever, freefall without end, until he woke screaming.

The insulated composite walls were extra thick on Kumeiijm'a, so no one came running. It wasn't just a dream. He knew that now. Looking down at his hands, he could feel the rough stone door's texture, remember the raised profile of the sigils that his fingers had brushed over.

For whatever use that was.

Waiting outside the Bar the next morning, Neroy was starting to worry Katyr wasn't coming. He shoved his hand in his pocket and gave the De'Spyr Shylling he still carried a rub, for good luck.

Shouts erupted from somewhere close by.

Seconds later a battered landCrawler skidded around the corner at high speed, heading straight for him. This early and the street wasn't crowded, but the hulking vehicle still came dangerously close to flattening a group of pedestrians, who only avoided being crushed under its enormous wheels by throwing themselves aside when it became clear the Crawler wasn't stopping. Neroy kept expecting it to slow down, but it didn't.

He stepped back into the lee of the building and retreated a few meters. The squeal of brakes merged with the screaming of tires on ice. He waited a moment, then poked his head out. The juddering Crawler had stopped at a forty-five-degree angle to the Bar, jutting out across the road. Its low-lying form had a brutal, military feel, armoured plates curving up to form a series of segmented domes that rested on six huge, black wheels, each one taller than Neroy. An access hatch slid open, and Katyr appeared.

"Move it," she growled. "Your creds covered some of my more life-threatening debts. But the other guys I owe aren't going to form an orderly queue when they hear there's money around."

"Some of my favourite people are creditors," smiled Neroy as he climbed in. "I've always made an effort to collect as many as possible."

Neroy barely had time to strap in before they tore out of Kay-City with as much speed as Katyr could hammer out of the engines. She kept it under manual control, driving with angry concentration. The Crawler was her brother's, on long term loan, and she proved adept at handling it as they rumbled through the tight City streets.

The warm, sour air of the cab started to make him feel nauseous. From the tangle of padding and blankets in the back, Neroy guessed she'd been living in it during her excavations. Printouts and dataPads were crammed-in everywhere, mostly site schematics, but science, history and philosophy were also well-represented. It was a tattered library, all torn pages and chipped screens. But it was clearly cherished.

The City fell behind them as they drove out into the vast whiteness covering the planet. Neroy gazed through the tinted windows at the endless ice, reflecting on the unlikeness of Katyr's discovery simply coinciding with his own re-emergence. There was something out there for him. He could feel it.

After a while they passed one last outpost where distant, tiny miners grappled with a vast and filthy machine. Then they left all trace of humanity behind. He'd never made it out this far on his previous visit. Too busy with his scheme in town. The one that had gotten him into so much trouble. He smiled. Still, it wasn't often he came up with something that affected the lives of every adult on a planet. Even if it was in ways some of their doctors wouldn't applaud.

The Crawler had a small flock of tethered drones that were tracking them, half a click above. Data from their camera feeds was spraying across the dashboard screens, the consensus from their real-time surveying of the local icefield merging with the navGuide to produce a pale pink driving lane for Katyr to follow, digitally painted onto the Crawler's windscreen by the AR systems. It was a dynamic display, constantly updating. The road before them twitched and shifted moment-by-moment, an artificial mirage that was the only dependable feature in a featureless landscape.

Looking at it wasn't doing anything for Neroy's stomach, so he focused on a small screen displaying a simple shot of them from above, a dark, bullish presence, carving through the blaze like a black ship in a white sea. A long time passed. Then something at the top of the screen snagged his attention. There, at the fringes, dark spots were starting to appear. Still some way ahead, the landscape was beginning to change.

Neroy gestured outside the Crawler, tracking his hand across the virginal expanse from arbitrary start-point through to random conclusion. "You know, out here, it just doesn't look like a planet where people have lived for centuries. Despite all the crap you can see from orbit."

Katyr grunted. "People still haven't touched most of the surface. Kumeiijm'a's almost twice as big as Earth." She stabbed a sideways look at him. 'And that crap you can see from orbit? That was all strip-mined for EarthFed's benefit. Didn't do the environment here any good, I can tell you that!"

"What environment? This place is solid ice!"

"You offworlders are all the same! Ignorant, and glad of it. We have oceans here, you know, under the frozen surface. We got tundra, down at the equator. Even out here, topography's all over the place." She glared at him. "Kumeiijm'a's a whole lot more than ice, Sphinx. As you're about to see."

Neroy shrugged. "Sorry. Guess I didn't really get out of Kay-City, last time I was here."

"You Earthers never do! Just come and visit your grateful little colony, and take what you need. And then leave."

"Unless I missed something on the news, those days are gone. EarthFed's fallen apart. There are no colonies anymore."

She snorted. "Believe that, you'll believe anything. Earth's been oppressing my people ever since they dumped them here, then made them totally dependent on supply lines we can't control."

Neroy started to regret having spoken. "Is that right? I've never been interested in politics."

Real anger flared in her voice. "You can afford not to be! Do you have any idea how things work here? EarthFed was all based around your planet reaching out through the wormholes a couple of hundred years ago, like some evil goddamn octopus. Mostly, they found existing human worlds. There were only ever a few actual colonies, like here. Places where humanity died out during the Isolation Aeons, and EarthFed started things up again. But it was all for Earth's benefit—they never wanted places like Kumeiijm'a to be independent, let alone equals!"

Neroy grinned. "Yeah? So tell me—how you people doing, without the EarthFed oppressor holding you back?"

Katyr seemed about to reply, then just exhaled angrily. She returned her focus to the way ahead. He couldn't blame her for feeling the way she did. Earth's formal remit didn't run any further than Neptune these days, and the worlds formerly under its influence had been left to their own devices, with the former Earth colonies largely struggling and impoverished.

Unlike worlds with non-Earth human populations, they generally didn't have a significant resource base to fall back on. Even after a couple of centuries, their societies lacked depth. In many ways the non-Earth worlds were better off than before, enjoying the continued benefits of interstellar trade with new room for political manoeuvre. But Earth had no successor, with the remnants of its agencies providing the only basis for the few interstellar socioeconomic systems that endured. Surviving institutions like the Orbitals now operated on a localised, autonomous basis beyond the Sol System, although coordination remained. But never in a way that seemed to allow the colonists to cut the cord, and better themselves.

Time to display some understanding. "I'm sorry, Katyr," Neroy said. "Didn't mean to be provocative. I know it's tough here. But seems to me there's an important difference between the Isolation Aeons, and now. None of us knows who ruled—and how—way back when. And we all know how EarthFed worked. Or didn't. But now?" He paused, waiting until she glanced over. "But now—maybe we're entering a Third Age. A new era, where things might be a little different. And we need to be prepared."

"Amen to that." She smiled, strangely. "But believe me. What we're about to see? No one's ready for that."

The mountain's peak rose up through the ice in an eruption of black, jagged rock. The angles of its dark crags seemed tormented, like the ossified hand of a giant that had died in agony, reaching up beyond the shroud of ice that entombed its titanic corpse.

Foreboding settled-in on Neroy as they approached, the pink thread in front of the Crawler twisting and turning as the fissures multiplied around the base of the mountaintop. They parked at the bottom of a relatively gentle slope, then scrambled up the obsidian scree until the Crawler was left far below. Neroy climbed in silence, exertion stealing his breath away. Katyr kept her pace slow to avoid getting too far ahead. As they neared the top of the slope, darkness began to fall, casting deep shadows that quickly bled into a murk that did nothing to lift Neroy's mood.

Just before they covered the final stretch, Katyr stopped. She gestured across the features of a gloomy landscape Neroy could only barely make out. "This here's the outlier, but keep heading east and you'll hit a whole mountain range. The peaks break through the ground ice pretty frequent, but they're easy to miss on account of how they're all frosted over. Just look like big icy mounds."

Neroy kicked a small rock loose. He watched it bounce down the scree until it disappeared into the dark, a rising wind snatching away any sound of its continued descent.

"Yeah?" he asked. "So why's this one different?"

The wind was picking up. Katyr had to shout to be heard. "The energy signature I told you about—it's coming from inside the mountain! Generating enough heat to melt the ice!"

"Enough to uncover a whole mountain?" yelled Neroy. That didn't sound good.

"No—we're just seeing the peak! The ice is over a kay deep at this point, almost all of it's under the surface." Katyr pulled at his arm. "Come on! Wind's getting worse—we need to get inside. Now!"

A quick upwards scramble took them to a broad ledge. For a moment Neroy couldn't see where they were heading, then a black fissure resolved out of the dark. Katyr disappeared inside, leaving Neroy alone in the howling, frigid night. With a backwards glance, he hurried after.

The darkness inside the fissure was total. Neroy fumbled for his torch, before a dim light came on somewhere deeper inside. He stumbled slowly forward and emerged into the cave itself. Katyr's headlamp cast enough illumination for him to make out the shape of the place, but little more. He couldn't see where it ended, but the part they were in was two or three times the size of the Crawler, empty aside from a stack of equipment Katyr was bent over, her light sweeping across it, searching for something.

"The hell were you thinking, leaving me out there?" he demanded.

"Sorry," she called, not turning around. "Thought I'd scoot ahead and get the lights turned on, but these goddamn power cells, you know? Control relays have frozen-over."

"I thought you said it was melting hot in here!"

"Warm enough to melt the ice on the surface, yeah. Over time, anyhow. But I wouldn't change into your swimsuit just yet."

"Just as well. I forgot to pack one. Luckily I swim naked."

"Yeah? That's a nauseating thought. Listen, I think I just need to-"

The lights blazed on in a pulse of illumination. Neroy screwed his eyes shut, steadying himself against the wall. As he blinked his tears away, the cave came into focus.

From the rear wall, an entrance tunnel beckoned. It was clearly artificial. Something about it was wrong in a way he couldn't define, but which seemed both obscene and at the same time disturbingly familiar. The curvature of the tunnel's entrance appeared to bend in on itself in a way that didn't quite fit the three-dimensional space in which it was embedded, giving it the quality of an optical illusion. Then the effect ceased, and it was just a tunnel entrance.

Neroy looked to Katyr, but she was still bent over her equipment. The fissure-end of the cave held a scattering of mining gear, along with life support equipment and a small shelter. She'd obviously spent time here before. But it was clearly just a staging post.

"So this is where you started off, right?" asked Neroy.

Katyr straightened up. "Yeah. Took me a couple weeks to unplug the entrance. I could only lug light gear up from the Crawler, so it was real slow going." She patted two squat grey cylinders that stood next to the shelter. "At least, until I brought these guys back from Kay-City." A small green light had begun to pulse on top of each cylinder. "Give them a minute, they're still booting up."

A scattering of indicator lights winked on across the surface of each drone. To a soundtrack of rapid clicks, their smooth surfaces cracked open, hairline fissures swiftly widening to reveal plates and segments that quickly shifted into a new, more practical configuration. Now with an ellipsoid shape, their fans started up and they rose into the air with a thrumming whine.

"There's my boys," Katyr smiled, patting the nearest one's armoured plating. "Come on. Let's get moving. Time to punch in for the first shift."

Katyr handed Neroy a powerful hand torch, and they entered the gently sloping tunnel. The floor was natural rock but the walls had a biological feel to them, with sets of rib-like spars rising up from the ground on each side to curve together overhead. One drone floated up front extending the bubble of light, but not to the extent that Neroy could see very far.

Immediately, anxiety kicked in. The unmistakeable feeling that something was waiting down below. There was a foul taste of adrenalin in his mouth, and his bowels were distinctly unhappy. Neroy glanced at Katyr but she was busy with her control tablet. He was suddenly struck by an unusually clear sense of where he was, at that precise moment in time. In a place that was smooth and frozen on the surface with a hidden past beneath, tempting to explore, but dangerous. He smiled. Looked at that way, it seemed like a metaphor.

Blurry points of angry red light sprayed across the tunnel wall.

"What the hell's that?" Neroy yelped.

"Sorry, sorry!" Katyr fiddled with her tablet until the red lines abruptly resolved themselves into something resembling a blueprint. It was a digital map, slithering along the wall next to them, keeping pace as they resumed their descent. "OK, the blue dots are us," she said, pointing a gloved hand to the top of the schematic. "Solid red lines are the sections I've managed to access, and the dotted lines are the AI's projection of what the layout of the rest of the place could be."

Neroy studied it. Two things were immediately apparent. The scale of the complex was vast, extending far down onto the mountain. And Katyr had barely scratched the surface of it. The solid reds only extended down two levels, encompassing what looked like a couple of main areas. Their tunnel ran from the cave entrance down to an initial sizeable chamber, and then on to a lower, smaller space.

As his eyes drifted over the dotted, postulated sections, something unpleasant occurred to him. Just as with the rib-spars in the tunnel, there was a disturbingly organic feel to the overall pattern. An invasive one. It looked like a cancer, some foul parasite burrowing its tendrils into the mountain.

"How old is this joint?" He wasn't sure he really wanted to know the answer.

"Kumeiijm'a's been on ice a long, long time. Sterile, pretty much. But being in a freezer preserves stuff, right? Keeps it unchanged. So places like this don't get overwritten by subsequent civilisations." She traced her fingers along the tunnel wall. "I've carbon dated some samples. Nothing definitive, but this place's at least a hundred thousand years old. That's around how long the wormhole system was down for." She craned her neck, looking up to where the rib-spars they were passing arched across the ceiling. "Place has been undisturbed ever since."

A sudden motion caught Neroy's eye. The map resolution was poor in this section of the tunnel but it looked like a third blue dot was moving beneath them, in the larger chamber.

"Katyr! There's something active down there!"

In the second it took for Katyr to turn around, the dot blinked out. Neroy pointed insistently at the second chamber's outline. "You leave another drone on the lower level or something?"

She snorted. "What, you think I'm made of money? There's nothing down there but cold and dark."

"Now that's a cheery thought. But seriously. There was another dot."

Her eyelids flickered as she reviewed the data stream from the relay sensors she'd installed, deployed across the areas she'd previously accessed. "Ah, it's probably just a glitch. This equipment's real old..."

"*Probably*? In my line of work, *probably's* a great way to get yourself killed."

She raised an eyebrow. "Yeah? And what kind of work would that be, exactly, Sphinx? You never did say."

Neroy smiled. "Supply Management." He held up a hand. "But please don't ask me to talk about it. It's pretty dull, really." Inside, Neroy wasn't smirking. Back on Deneb IV, he'd been certain Bukowski's S&M revelations related to Kumeiijm'a somehow. It was what had brought him here. But now he didn't feel so sure.

Katyr sent both drones up ahead, extending the forward light bubble by several metres. She shrank the map back to their Heads Up Displays, which Neroy kept maximised as they continued to descend. He lowered his hood and removed his visor as the air warmed slightly. Before long, they reached the first chamber.

It was vast. The lights from the drones gave a tentative sense of the overall dimensions, without dispelling the shadowy edges. Hewn from the living rock of the mountain, it had the feel of some ancient, crumbling temple. There were flagstones underfoot, and soaring columns lurked on the fringes of the chamber. But time had emptied it of whatever it had originally held. Endless piles of frigid debris covered the floor.

Neroy squatted down to inspect the nearest mound. He scooped up a handful of debris, letting the gritty fragments drain through the fingers of his thermSuit. "Not much left, is there? This stuff could have been anything. Machinery. Weapons. Maybe it's all that's left of whoever lived here..."

Katyr was checking one of her relay sensors. He walked over to join her.

"Hardly the discovery of a lifetime so far, is it?" Neroy said. "Not unless you lead a pretty dull life, I guess."

She grunted, then sent a command to the drones. They started drifting towards the far end of the chamber, taking their bubble of light with them.

"Didn't say this was it, did I, Sphinx? Lower level's far better preserved. Come on."

They moved off across the stone floor, following in the wake of the drones. The mounds weren't dense but walking through them made a mess of the thermSuits, so they drifted to the near side of the chamber where the way was clearer. Halfway to the back of the hall they came across a spiral twist of stonework the size of a human statue, broken-off millennia ago from some larger piece. It was covered with glyphs, but as the details emerged from the gloom Neroy found that it hurt to look at them too closely. He averted his eyes as they passed.

"Come on. I know you're dying to tell me. Who do you think built this place?"

"Well, there's no simple answer to that. But I've had a whole lot of time down here to think about it." She looked at him. "I'm going to assume you don't know much about pre-Isolation historical theories, right?"

Neroy was about to gesture for her to continue, but she ploughed on before he got that far. Her tone was different from before. More rapid-fire, more unapologetically passionate, slipping now into a detailed fluency at odds with how she'd previously talked about the place.

"Well, archaeological records are limited, obviously. But they suggest humanity used to be part of a wider meta-civilisation, including intelligent non-human entities."

"Aliens, right?" said Neroy. "You mean aliens?"

"Aliens. Yeah. But there was then a cataclysmic war. It disrupted the wormhole system, leaving deep scars that are still healing."

"Yeah, even I know that. Not sure I learned about ancient aliens in school, though."

"No one does." For a moment, she smiled strangely. "The evidence is too slight, too disputed. But whatever came before us, everyone assumes the war destroyed any other intelligent species that may have existed. And we've never found any. Even before EarthFed, humanity scanned the stars with Radio Telescopes. Primitive, but effective. But there were never any results. Whole programme got dumped."

"Honestly? People really did that?"

"Yeah, Sphinx. People really did that. Now, as a wise woman once said, absence of evidence isn't evidence of absence. But, yeah. Everyone assumes humanity's alone, at least in the current era."

They'd drifted closer to the wall and the intermittent columns were now under ten metres away. Neroy glanced at them. Their proximity made him uncomfortable.

"So you're saying aliens built this joint?" asked Neroy, looking away. "Well, OK. So where are they now?"

She shrugged. "Like I said, current mainstream thinking is they got wiped out in the conflict that kicked-off the Isolation. But I don't think that was the end of the story."

"Just right now, I'd prefer a story with a happy ending. You know, to brighten things up a little. Is this going to be one of those?"

"Depends on your perspective," growled Katyr. "Look, you paid me to bring you here. Against my better judgement. So now we're here. And you asked me who I thought built it. So I'm telling you. I didn't invite you here, and I'm not a goddamn tour guide."

Neroy stopped, obliging her to halt as well. He held up his hands. "Sorry. Listen, I appreciate everything you're doing. Straight up. Please—sincerely—tell me what you were going to say."

They resumed walking, in silence.

"...well, not much to tell, really," said Katyr, after a while. "From what I've heard, the wormhole system's theorised to spread across the wider galaxy. Not just the Human Systems. So it was only the branch in Earth's quadrant of the Milky Way that completely burned out in the war, cutting us off. The rest of galactic civilisation presumably just carried right on, while we all rotted in a local stone age for a few millennia. And the culture that built this place? They're probably still out there."

Neroy didn't want another bust-up. But what she was saying implied another layer here. A link to something wider and deeper. Maybe something that ultimately connected to him. He coughed, needlessly. "Katyr, I'm curious. Not just about the historical stuff—but how do you actually know all this? Isn't it a little above the pay grade of a renegade miner, out in the frozen ass-end of nowhere? Even a very well-read one," he added, "who's clearly a hell of a lot smarter than I am."

She sniffed. Needlessly, as far as he could tell. "I read stuff, you know? From specialist institutions like the GAI on Cassiopia. And I sell the artefacts I find to a few different buyers," she said. "But the regulars are part of the Candrassian Order. You ever heard of them?"

"Well, sure. Bunch of religious kooks. Charitable works, privy to ancient mysteries, yadda yadda yadda."

"There's a whole lot more to them than that, Sphinx, although they don't tend to advertise it. Or at least there is to some of them. Depends on which faction. But the Activist sects within the Order? They've got some of the deepest pockets around."

"Is that right? Maybe I ought to get to know them a little better."

"Good luck with that. The ones I know are pretty choosy about the types of non-believers they're prepared to hang out with."

"Let me guess—they're prepared to be more flexible if you happen to have something they want?"

She smirked. "You guessed it. And sometimes that's me. And when it is, I drive the hardest bargain I can. They pay me what I want, and, if I have to hand over something fascinating I'd rather keep a hold of, the least they can do is tell me as much as they know about what makes it so goddamn special. After a while, all those little snippets add up to scraps of something bigger." Neroy nodded approvingly. Knowing the value of what you had was the first step in making someone else pay more than they wanted to for it. He was about to say as much, when a blur of motion caught his eye.

Something had moved at the edge of the chamber.

Neroy scanned the columns. As he did, they seemed to recede into an infinite grey darkness. Vertigo struck, making him stagger, but Katyr caught him before he fell.

"I—I saw something move..." was all he could manage.

Katyr whistled an override command. The drones swooped back to hover above them, spotlights trained on the side wall. There was a rough alcove, coated in dripping ice that was frosted over the rock. Katyr examined the ground.

"No tracks through the debris field except ours. Must have been the melting ice you saw. Come on." She pulled him with her. "Not far to the next tunnel now."

"I'd prefer a story with a happy ending."

They soon reached the rear wall of the chamber. There were three tunnel entrances, but only the one on the right was accessible, the others blocked by ancient rockfalls. The drones went ahead, and Katyr projected her AR map on the tunnel wall again. The angle was steeper now, the descent quicker. Before long, they emerged into another echoing chamber.

The difference was immediately apparent. It was a smaller space down here, the light from the drones reaching every corner, revealing intricate carvings on the walls that meant nothing to Neroy, but which generated a sense of foreboding he did his best to ignore. There was a heap of mining gear at the tunnel mouth, left in preparation for an assault on a huge stone door. It was sealed, not blocked by rock-falls, but there was no obvious way of opening it. Hieroglyphic symbols curved over the portal in a mighty arc, the faded script of giants.

"End of the line for now, huh?" said Neroy. "So what's down here? This where you found all the good stuff?"

"Yeah, so far. The artefacts on this layer are much better preserved, along with the stonework. Whatever damaged the upper level? It must not have penetrated this far down." Katyr walked to the far side of the chamber, the droids following, casting a brighter light in front of her. What had previously looked like darker areas of rock were revealed to be small side chambers. Neroy joined her in the furthest alcove. There were traces of metallic frames that could have been cradles, or seats. Scattered over the floor were a variety of blackened, broken objects, around the size of a human head. Neroy picked one up. It was a skeletal thing, spindly legs spreading out from a central mass. There was something unnatural about its curving lines that made it unpleasant to look at.

"They're always burnt like that," she said. "Everything I find. Always. Must have been that ancient war."

"Maybe," shrugged Neroy, thinking back to Dubblz' briefing files on the portal generator back in TC. "But the people who collect things like these—the stuff may be ruined, but they still manage to reverse-engineer some of it, sometimes." Neroy put it down gently, exactly where he'd found it. "And then we end up with portals, chamCloaks—Exotic Tech. I've come across stuff like that before." Indeed he had. And apparently he'd been tangled up in the whole thing, years ago, right up to his neck. In places exactly like this, for all he knew. Supply Management indeed. Maybe his instincts back on Deneb IV had been right about Kumeiijm'a after all.

She nodded, then came over and stared down at the artefact he'd just examined. "I'd love to meet the people involved in all that, not just my contacts. They must be fascinating."

"Yes, yes, they must be," Neroy nodded. "But even they don't seem to understand the tech fully. At least not well enough to make it easy to use." He thought of the Cloak he'd had to dump after Deneb IV. "No way of recharging the tech they make from it with regular power systems. That I know of, anyhow."

Neroy sensed Katyr's hesitation.

"My contact in the Candrassian Order told me about that," she offered tentatively. "But you wouldn't want to know about it, would you? Religious kooks, you called them." She looked offended, but carried on. "He called it *Soul Fuel.*"

"Well, that does sound just a little like a phrase a religious kook would use. What does it mean?"

She was annoyed now. "He was a condescending ass. I'm pretty sure the jerk didn't really understand it either. But once, I got him to talk about all that reverse-engineered Exotic Tech you mentioned. When I had a real good haul he wanted."

Neroy drifted towards the next alcove, Katyr falling in step with him. One of the drones dipped lower to light their path with a milky luminescence that drifted over the cracked stone flags like mist. Katyr started up with a torrent of thoughts Neroy felt she'd probably been keeping to herself for far too long.

"The tech these artefacts allow people to make," she began, "it seems to break physical laws. To do things it shouldn't be able to. Like move from A to B without travelling the distance in-between, but without using a natural wormhole. Or to be unseen by human eyes, but also undetectable by computers. Apparently? My guy said it's some form of quantum tech, linked to exotic particles. That somehow link back to us, the conscious beings who use the tech. It's a two-way thing, you know? Consciousness-related effects that also impact the physical world. You know your history of physics at all?"

She pushed on without waiting for an answer. "Schrodinger's Cat. Observers, under the right conditions, influence external phenomena. Cause it, in a witnessing-stuff-makes-it-happen sense, I guess. Somehow, there's a form of consciousness-manipulation of quantum processes involved. Giving dead matter a nudge. That's apparently what makes this stuff work, somehow. On an industrial scale, I'd imagine. You can't just plug it into a fusion reactor."

Neroy had been around enough psychics to know that the human mind was a powerful thing. But this?

"What, some kind of *attention energy* or something?" He picked up another blackened artefact and stared at it. "Well, I'm paying real close attention, but nothing so far. Maybe it's bust."

She scowled. "Maybe. Or maybe you're a moron."

The next alcove was empty aside from deep carvings in the stone. Katyr pointed to the largest set of patterns. Neroy recognised the planets of the

Kumeiijm'a System. Other markings surrounded the planetary System, focusing on two web-like symbols set some way off from the planets themselves.

"See?" said Katyr, excitedly. "This is what I was saying yesterday, in the bar! It's a stellar map—this System actually has two wormholes. One we know about..."

"...and another one," concurred Neroy. It seemed obvious, somehow, although he didn't know why. Rather than being pleased with his agreement Katyr seemed annoyed, as if cheated out of a moment of revelation she'd been anticipating. Neroy ignored her as he examined more of the carvings. Most of them meant nothing. But one, a simple icon, was strangely familiar. Unlike most of the incomprehensible squiggles, it seemed to be a picture of a real object. A burning sun, with a vertical bar across its central circle.

It was one of the icons from his nightmare back in the habWarren.

A slow *twisting* gripped his stomach, as though someone had reached deep inside and grabbed a handful of his guts. Something was stirring within the Cold Black Glass, brushing up against it from the other side.

Nothing good.

"Hey, come see what I've got here," called Katyr, from the next alcove. He clung to her voice, a lifeline, as he staggered to join her. The spotlights from the drones were pointing down at her, a shimmering, angelic figure in the darkness. She smiled like a wolf as he reached her, and the lights swept past her to illuminate a huge figure that towered above them both.

A monster.

Neroy stared at it in dumb horror, a jumble of crazed impressions fighting to cohere into something that made biological sense. Bipedal, but with an insectoid, crustacean look. The creature had enormous crablike claws, with a chitinous, wedge-shaped torso and huge bulbous eyes that protruded above a gaping maw crammed with tusk-like teeth.

The blackness in his gut twisted *hard,* and he was lost. He wasn't inside the mountain anymore, he was somewhere infinitely cold and infinitely vast. Somewhere that was too big, too black. Somehow he could sense he was out amongst the stars, but he was also beyond them, too far away from them to ever see their light, too small and insignificant ever to be found again, lost, lost utterly.

A howling laughter swept in from the darkness, surrounding him, draping itself over him until he was even more lost, but no longer alone. Now it was even worse, now there was something terrible with him, there in the void. The terror clawed its way down his throat, choking him, but he could still scream and he began to howl, a desperate, screeching wail that-

Something hit his face very hard, and then he was scrabbling on the gritty chamber floor. Light from the drones burned a tight white circle around him.

"What the hell was that?" yelled Katyr. "Stop screaming! What's wrong with you?!"

Neroy flopped onto his ass and spat out a wad of bloody saliva. He blinked slowly, rubbing his jaw. "Did you just punch me?"

"You... you were hysterical! I couldn't make you stop, I-"

Neroy held out his hand. Katyr hesitated, then hauled him up. She looked very concerned. He couldn't really blame her.

"Listen, I'm sorry I hit you, man..."

Neroy stared at the statue. "What... what *is* that thing?"

Katyr scratched pensively at the back of her head. "Ah, shit. I just wanted to be a little, you know, dramatic."

He walked past her, drawn to the creature.

"Magnificent, isn't it?" she said. "I've never seen anything like it. No one has, I don't think."

He remembered the dream from the night before, and the sigils he'd seen in it. There, at the base of the statue, was a series of tiny stone tiles. Almost like buttons. Each bore an icon in some indecipherable alien lexicon. None of them meant anything.

Except the three that he remembered.

Twisted spiral>Burning sun>Broken pyramid.

He reached out a trembling hand. Slowly, he extended his index finger.

"...ah, Sphinx, what are you doing, man?" asked Katyr. There was a note of concern in her voice. He could sense her reaching out to restrain him.

Too late.

He pressed the three sigils quickly in sequence. The action seemed to wake him up, to snap him out of something. "Uh, Katyr? I really don't know what I'm up to, here. Just thought I should make that clear..."

In the darkness of the chamber, nothing happened.

"OK. Well, no harm done, I guess..." she said. "But listen, maybe we ought to think about heading-"

A hideous scream of words-that-weren't-language tore through the audio spectrum, driving them to their knees. Neroy clamped his hands over his ears as the barrage pummelled them. Subsonics battered his eardrums to the point of agony. The sound was coming from everywhere, with an intensity that made the floor seem like it was shaking.

The screeching suddenly stopped, and he realised the floor was shuddering. Not just the floor, but also the end-wall of the chamber where the sealed door was now slowly grinding open, loosing a cloud of frigid dust. Neroy staggered to his feet. The rumbling continued, then increased. A rain of pebbles and small rocks started falling from above. He heard Katyr screaming at him, but there was something behind the rising door that was calling to him more insistently. A dull, fiery glitter was rising in intensity just inside the threshold. Neroy had no idea what it was, but he knew that it was wonderful. The answers he needed. They were all there. He took a step forward, then another, aware on some level that rocks and chunks of ice were tumbling down from above. But it just didn't matter.

Then all he could see was red.

A mesh of annoying crimson lines had sprung up everywhere, getting in the way of the glittering. He couldn't focus on the glow behind the door properly. At first that angered him. Then he wondered why the glittering shapes had seemed so very important just a few seconds before. The red lines of the digital map shifted as the resolution adapted to his Heads Up Display. As the floor plan of the chamber snapped into focus, he became aware of Katyr shouting.

"-ucking coming up behind us! Move, you idiot!"

A third blue dot was approaching very rapidly from behind, heading straight for the azure circles representing Katyr and himself. Neroy had time to half-turn, then something small and dark shot past his feet, heading for the doorway. As it approached the entrance it slowed to a rapid scuttle, and in the flicker of light from within Neroy saw something small and skeletal, with spindly legs that propelled it across the rocky floor in a way that was profoundly unnatural. It vanished inside, and the door lowered behind it.

The shaking worsened dramatically. A huge rock fell from the chamber ceiling, hitting the ground nearby with a shocking impact. The rumbling increased again as they staggered towards the tunnel, ground bucking under their feet. One of the drones was smashed by falling debris, then the other's light went out too, throwing them into darkness.

Katyr switched the Heads Up to infrared and dragged Neroy after her as the world became a shuddering mist of black and crimson, strafed by falling lumps of rock. Somehow they reached the tunnel entrance, now partially blocked by debris. It looked passable, barely, but with a sudden crash an immense boulder fell from above, almost crushing them, wedging-in between them and the tunnel. Katyr screamed at him to move, but move where? There was a sound like thunder, and his head exploded with pain.

Then darkness.

The bumping of the Crawler slowly brought him round.

In the halfway space between unconsciousness and active thought, he knew he wasn't dead, but he was happy to hide from the throbbing in his head for as long as possible. Eventually, he forced his eyes open. Katyr had patched him up and dumped him on a mattress that, now he could see, he realised was heavily soiled. Shuffling off it without standing up made enough noise to attract her attention, but she stayed focused on the terrain ahead as she drove.

"What the hell were you doing, just standing around under a rock fall?" She sounded furious. "You got to find a reinforced space in a situation like that, wait it out. There was an alcove just off to the side!"

"Nice... to know you care."

"Yeah, well, screw that. You die in there, I don't get the rest of my money."

Neroy started to reply, but the thought of it exhausted him. He slumped back on the mattress and slept. Later, as night was falling, he joined her in the front of the cab. She told him what had happened.

Their escape had been simple enough. The disturbance had temporarily stabilised, shortly after what she assured him had been an embarrassingly small rock had knocked him out. She'd used the mining equipment to unblock the tunnel, then hooked him up to the surviving drone, still semi-functional, which had dragged him out. Just in time, as the seismic activity had then kicked back in, sealing the main access tunnel.

Neroy fell asleep again. When he woke, his head felt clearer. They sat in companionable silence for a time. Then she glanced at him, the orange glow of the dashboard highlighting a look of concern on her face. The expression softened her, he thought.

"Don't tell anyone what we saw," she said.

"Why not?" he replied. "It's not like you couldn't do with the tourists on this iceball."

"Maybe. But if the scale of what I found gets out—the possibility of the tech actually being active? Earth would send people to tear that place apart. There's no way they'd let me dig my way in again, maybe learn something more. Not if they get the scent of a goldmine. Their weapons industry, it's just too hungry. You know?"

He didn't know. That was the problem. But she was right, he was sure of it. Somewhere deep inside the Cold Black Glass they were all connected. The things he'd seen inside the mountain. The Military-Industrial Complex. Supply Management. The Fall of EarthFed.

And him.

Back in the Bar in Kay-City, they were well into their second bottle before Neroy realised he wanted her. They were sat at the same discrete corner table as before, where he could keep an eye on the entrance, just in case anyone he'd crossed during his previous job here happened to saunter in. He'd paid Katyr, but she wasn't in any hurry to leave. They'd been talking for a while now about everything they'd seen, everything that had happened. Whatever else might still be down there. What it might all mean.

But now the mood was suddenly sliding into something else.

Neroy reached for his glass but his hand kept on moving, and when it stopped he was holding hers. As soon as he'd done it he loosened his touch, to allow her to pull away. But she didn't. Instead Katyr slid her other hand over his, strong fingers flexing out to gently stroke his wrist.

"Wasn't expecting you to do that," she said, in a low voice.

"Neither was I. I guess... I guess we shared something back there."

She was searching for truth in the past and he wanted some of that, he realised. To touch someone else on a journey like his, if only for a moment. It wasn't trust, or love, or anything like that. Just a recognition of something sympathetic to his own nature. Something he understood, and which might understand him.

"I guess we did, Sphinx," she said. "It's lonely out there, sometimes."

"All the time, I'd guess."

"Maybe so," Katyr said. "And most of the time, that's OK."

She leaned across the table and put her hand behind his head, pulling his face towards her and kissing him on the mouth. "But that doesn't mean I have to like it."

In the half-light of his room they lay entwined, Katyr's taut, well-muscled miner's body curled into his skinnier frame, head resting on his chest. He sucked down a lungful of smoke. The closest to peace he'd known in a long time. Katyr took the Cig from him, blowing smoke down his stomach towards his navel. She handed it back and pulled the blankets tight around them both, settling in.

"So when were you here, before? Tell me about it. When was that, exactly?"

"Right after EarthFed fell apart, as it happens. I've kind of been retracing my steps."

"Oh, right. No one forgets where they were when that happened, do they?"

Neroy frowned. "Actually? I've no idea where I was when it went down. I woke up on Kumeiijm'a a few days afterwards with a hole in my memory you could drive a shuttle through. Met a beautiful woman who helped me get back on my feet, though…"

Katyr reached out for another drag. "Do I remind you of her?"

"Not really," said Neroy, accepting it back. "She didn't have your class."

He winced. What was presumably meant to be a playful punch in the ribs felt like it was going to leave a bruise.

"Oh, really," purred Katyr. "Why don't you tell me about it." She nestled her head back into the side of his chest. And in that moment, lights dimmed low, the scouring wind howling above them while the warmth of her body soaked into his, he thought, why not? That ancient place inside the mountain hadn't taught him much. Not really. But perhaps telling her what had happened before would shake something loose.

Perhaps it would just be good to talk.

"I'd been in hospital," Neroy began. "Not sure why. Before that, I don't remember anything. Not for a stretch of years."

"What, nothing?" asked Katyr. "Literally?

"No. Nothing at all. Big memory gap. And the hospital's pretty blurry too... first thing I really remember's being out in the cold, looking for a room and somewhere to get a drink. Then I met her, and we came here. To this bar."

"Her?" prompted Katyr.

"Said I could call her Ms Black. Met her out on the street, we just got talking. Turned out she didn't seem to feel the cold. Guess that was why she was hanging around out there."

"What did she look like?"

Neroy paused. Just as with the things he'd seen inside the mountain that had felt familiar, even though they couldn't have been. His memories of her somehow seemed like he was recalling meeting an old acquaintance. Someone he'd known well, even before their encounter on the ice planet. "Tall, blonde. Beautiful on the surface, but in the same way a predator looks perfect, right before it eats you."

"Sounds like she made quite an impression."

"Well, she was effectively the first person I'd met on the face of the planet. And we turned out to have a whole lot in common."

"Really? You're going grey, but it'd be a stretch to describe it as blonde. As for beautiful..."

"Turned out she wanted to get into my line of work, after we'd had a few drinks. I had a seriously lousy memory, but only for a certain period. Still knew my trade well enough. I threw out a few war stories that evening, and she lapped them up. Said she'd been engaged in something similar, but her employer had just cut her loose. Wanted to build up a little stake money, for some kind of research project."

Neroy frowned as he dredged up details from long ago. "She'd been some kind of, I don't know. Hired muscle. Operational support, that kind of thing. Very strong. Real tech-savvy, too. Genius-level. Maybe something military-related."

Katyr nodded. "The Company use specialist freelancers sometimes, to back up the sheriff crews. For stuff like union busting. There was a lot of that going on back then. Turbulent times."

"Yeah, she'd have been real good at that. Anyways, whatever she'd been up to, she was at a loose end. Like me. So we decided to do a job. Team up. She wanted to see how I did the magic, and I got some backup."

She raised an eyebrow, unimpressed. "Yeah? And what magic would that be, Sphinx?"

He smiled as he remembered. "She said I was a specialist. How did she put it? *An expert at making something out of nothing. Especially when that something belongs to someone else.*" He shrugged, as much as he was able to while lying down with someone draped over him. "What can I say… it's a gift. Anyway, she was eager to learn. Real eager." He frowned. "But she was a little different, neurologically speaking. Found it kind of hard to empathise. That's a challenge when it comes to working with marks, you know. Need to be able to get inside their heads."

"So how does it work, Sphinx?" asked Katyr. "How do you come up with an angle? If you want to make something out of nothing, which piece of nothing do you choose?"

Neroy nodded in a professorial way. "Good question. The only question, really. I'll admit the options can feel a little daunting, sometimes, when it's real open-ended. The tyranny of the blank rap sheet. But back then, I wasn't firing on all cylinders. Looked at one way, I was maybe a little lazy. Or you could say I took inspiration where I found it."

"Which means what, exactly? Don't keep me in suspense here."

"Well, you start with people. What do they want that they can't have? Everyone wants something for nothing. Everyone. Figure out what that is—and let them think they're getting the better of you—and you take it from there. Sitting in a bar in Kay-City a week after EarthFed fell apart, prices were spiking for everything from bar snacks to condoms. But booze and narcs especially. In times of change, people want stuff to help them forget, to smooth out the rough edges. And people on Kumeiijm'a? They love to drink, first and last and always."

"It's true. We're miners. Goes with the territory, all the way back to Old Earth times."

"So that was it. Everything here's either imported, or grown in a hydroChamber. Sky-high prices either way, once supply lines start getting all disrupted and stocks start getting a little thin."

Katyr rolled to the edge of the bed and fished inside one of her boots for a narcPack she'd stashed earlier. "So skip to the good part already. What was the scam?"

Neroy gave a loud mock-sigh. "People today, they got no patience. I was just building up to the big reveal." He waited for a put-down, but Katyr was busy inhaling from the Pack.

"Well, OK, I'll give you a clue. You ever read the Earth Bible?"

Katyr's nose was running. She managed to make sniffing loudly sound utterly disdainful. "Of course not."

Neroy leaned halfway out of bed and picked up her boot. There was still ice in the ridges of the sole. He dug a little out and held it up on the tip of his finger. "Well, one thing this planet does have is ice, and there's an old trick I always wanted to try. Kind of a miracle, actually."

Katyr shook her head, trying to follow him through the drug rush. "Sphinx... what are you talking about?"

"I asked her to turn water into wine. Well, beer, actually. Not much of a wine-drinking culture here. And it turned out she could. Well, close enough. Took her a week to figure out synthesising alcohol from non-fermented liquids." A look of frustration crossed his face. "Although the local water, it had the wrong sorts of trace metals, so we had to use... something else."

"What?"

Neroy winked at her. "Trade secret. Although I can exclusively reveal the supply was inexhaustible. After that, once we had the formula and the production process all down pat, it was just a matter of hammering out a deal with the local Mob."

He beamed at the memory. "Ms Black was a real effective negotiating partner. Anyway, we drove a hard bargain, and there was a little turbulence along the way. Broke a few eggshells to get the omelette made, you know how it goes. But the bootleggers we sold the process to? They were so fond of their own product I didn't think they'd live long enough to cause me grief if I ever came back."

A slow understanding sparked in Katyr's eyes. "That old guy in the bar, back when we first met... you panicked, disappeared as soon as he walked in."

Neroy looked rueful. "Well observed, Ms Yol. But yeah, that's right. Ms Black kind of removed his brother's trachea at a critical stage in the negotiations." He smiled. "Still, it did lead to the pivotal breakthrough."

Katyr was slowing down as the narc soaked through her nervous system. "Hey... but you must have walked away with a fortune, you know..."

Neroy lit a smoke. "Kind of an ambiguous statement there, Katyr. To be specific, it was less of the plural, more of the singular, I'm afraid, and the subject of the sentence was feminine, not masculine."

Katyr screwed her face up, annoyed. "What the hell... you talking about?"

"Just prior to my vast enrichment, Ms Black applied a nerve pinch to my carotid artery, liquidated our assets, and left me to wake up alone with a raging headache. And a sense of vast despair that had nothing to do with a hangover." He blew out a plume of smoke that slowly coiled up to the ceiling. "Never saw her again. But she was one of the most remarkable people I ever met. Leastways, as far as I remember..."

Katyr flopped down on the bed and pulled the covers up. "So... so what happened... next?"

"Nothing. Nothing happened next. I was stuck here on my ass. No money, but a lot of drinking. Things get a little blurrier after that. Guess I was hitting it hard. Got back to Earth somehow, then kicked back for a few years... well, ten... and now I'm here again. Full circle..."

Katyr stopped asking questions after that, just snuggled into his side, her breath stroking his chest. Neroy hadn't taken a narc, but a slow warmth started spreading through his body too.

And then, in that unanticipated moment of peace, he relaxed enough that something realigned in his mind. Not a *twist*, nothing jarring. Just a shift of balance so that something became obvious, as though it had always been sitting in plain sight but he just hadn't noticed it before. Ms Black was someone he'd met prior to the hospital ten years ago, he was suddenly certain. An acquaintance from within the era of the Cold Black Glass. Someone who'd then sought him out when he was vulnerable, lost to himself, to get something she wanted, but couldn't ask from him before.

The realisation brought a feeling of relief he couldn't explain, but felt no need to question. He'd come to Kumeiijm'a for answers. He hadn't really found any, but this would do until something better came along.

Neroy dressed quickly in the semi-darkness. He'd overslept, but there was still just enough time to make today's last Orbital shuttle. Transports had become less frequent lately, with captains growing skittish at reports of local ships disappearing.

Neroy turned around and saw Katyr smiling up at him. She didn't want him to stay, didn't need him any more than he needed her. But still. It felt as close to affection as he'd been in years.

"So where you heading next, Sphinx?" she asked, grabbing her jumpsuit and rooting around for her boots.

It was a good question. Maybe it was time for Cassiopia. It was the only place that really had a mature data culture equivalent to Earth or Deneb IV, both of which were off-limits for now. So someone on Cassiopia would probably have access to detailed records on S&M. And there'd be some pricey Psych Clinic there to open up his memories instead, if not. Cassiopian med-tech was second to none. With their extensive cloning industry, they were experts on cognitive systems. So they should be good at repair jobs too. But before he headed there, he should kick back a little. For one thing, he needed to shake off the effects of the beating he'd taken under the mountain. The pain in his head had retreated to a dull throb, but it was still enough to make him wince.

"Cassiopia. But not right away. First, I deserve a break. Somewhere a little warmer than this place." He smiled. Kaalis, perhaps. A resort world could be just the ticket. And Kaalis was only a short transit away.

"Well, jeez, thanks, that narrows it down." Katyr pushed past him to the tiny bathroom cubicle. "Gimme a minute, I got to pee before I burst." She slid the door shut and sat down noisily.

As Neroy fumbled with his thermSuit he thought back to the mountain. Looked at one way, he'd only succeeded in collecting pieces that still didn't fit together—Supply Management, the Fall of EarthFed, the trade in ancient Artefacts and all the rest of it. But he had to acknowledge there was more than that, now. His nightmares related to something real, something ancient that connected to everything he couldn't remember. Something tangible, and somehow familiar. Something he could reach out and touch. That had to count as progress, but whether it was taking him closer to something good or something awful, he just couldn't say.

He snapped the last clasp shut on his thermSuit and checked his belongings. The stars awaited. And somewhere amongst them were the answers he needed, just waiting to be picked from someone's pocket.

A flushing noise came from the bathroom, then Katyr was calling out to him. "Listen, you sure I can't tempt you to grab a quick beer before you leave? I'm buying."

Neroy thought about the catchment tanks Ms Black had designed that looped back to the brewing vats through an intricate series of filters. Given how robust she'd designed the mechanics to be, they probably hadn't needed to replace any of the parts, even after ten years.

"No thanks, honey. It kind of loses its appeal if you know where it comes from."

THE END

for Barbara, Anna, Max and Oscar

ABOUT OUR CREATORS

WRITER –

DANIEL WHISTON is a Learning Designer whose day job involves writing online educational content. He's also the bass player in the rock band Mighty Dynamite. As a scriptwriter, his "explainer animations" and videos have been produced extensively for the BBC and others. His *Neroy Sphinx: Back in the Game* graphic novel was published by FutureQuake Press, with its follow-up *Neroy Sphinx: Playing to Lose* published by Markosia. Comics written by him have also appeared in *Judge Dredd Megazine, Sliced Quarterly, Dead By Dawn,* and *Shock-a-Rama.* His comicbook stories featuring the 2000AD stable of characters have featured in multiple issues of *Zarjaz, Dogbreath* and the Eagle Award-nominated *FutureQuake.* He is also the co-creator of Gideon Gunn from Richmond Press. Daniel's interview with Alan Moore was published in *Alan Moore: Conversations* from the University Press of Mississippi. His next title from Airship 27 will be *Amongst the Crooked Stars.* He lives in Bath, England.

COVER ART & ILLUSTRATIONS –

DAVE THOMSON - is a Graphic Designer from Edinburgh, Scotland, with a passion for European comics. His art has appeared in many independent titles in the UK including *Dr WTF, The Psychedelic Journal of Time Travel, 100% Biodegradeable* and *Zarjaz.* He took over art duties for *Neroy Sphinx in FutureQuake* over a decade ago and has been drawing his adventures ever since!

{-BEFORE METROPOLIS-}

In 1927 German filmmaker Fritz Lang brought to the screen one of the most ground-breaking sci-fi melodramas of all time based on the screenplay he co-wrote with his wife, novelist Thea von Harbou. Set in a futuristic urban dystopia, the story follows the attempts of Freder, the son of the city's ruler, and Maria, a citizen of the lower levels, to bridge the gulf separating the economic classes of the city. It is regarded as a classic and one of the first full-length movies in the genre.

In a new series of anthologies from Airship 27 Productions today's best New Pulp writers explore the world of Metropolis prior to the classic film. Join the excitement and suspense in THE TOWERS OF METROPOLIS!

Airship27Hangar.com

Pulp Fiction for a New Generation!

www.ingramcontent.com/pod-product-compliance
Lightning Source LLC
LaVergne TN
LVHW010922110826
845149LV00013B/2452